SPIDERSILK

© COPYRIGHT 2013-2025

EIGHTH EDITION

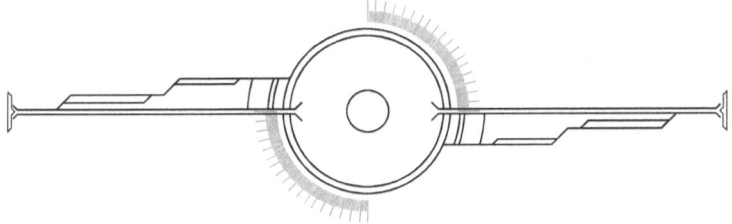

Akutra-Ramses Atenosis Cea

Copyright © 2013-2025 by Akutra-Ramses Atenosis Cea

First edition 03/27/2013,

Second edition 08/21/2013,

Third Edition 11/26/2015,

Fourth Edition 10/09/2018,

Fifth Edition 7/5/2021,

Sixth Edition 8/26/2023,

Seventh Edition 03/24/2025,

Eighth Edition 10/06/2025

ISBN: 978-1-990695-18-6 (Paperback)

978-1-990695-19-3 (E-book)

All rights reserved. No part of this publication may be reproduced, distributed, or transmitted in any form or by any means, including photocopying, recording, or other electronic or mechanical methods, without the prior written permission of the publisher, except in the case brief quotations embodied in critical reviews and other noncommercial uses permitted by copyright law.

The views expressed in this book are solely those of the author and do not necessarily reflect the views of the publisher, and the publisher hereby disclaims any responsibility for them.

BookSide Press
877-741-8091
www.booksidepress.com
orders@booksidepress.com

Contents

Introduction 1

Moving In 3

Blast from the Past. 19

Tragic Leap 35

The Party 49

Contact 71

Investigations. 85

Friends 107

Meet the New Contractor 121

Not Your Typical Fight 139

Gone Missing. 159

Dueling Forces. 173

The Returning. 189

Closure and Revelation 208

Afterword 223

Introduction

WELCOME TO OLYMPUS, an alternate world similar yet different to Earth. Mark Kheops, a tech-savvy video game developer, has the secret ability of connecting to entangled worlds and must foil the plans of abducting intruders while exploring other worlds. Mark is a stylishly slick and highly skilled video game developer with a few extra abilities and an army of spiders in a parallel universe.

Nearly everything is a mysterious connection "to something," the dream landscape blends with reality when Mark inadvertently connects to a world on the cusp of a black hole, opening the door to new and unusual entities. However, not everyone is friendly, as Mark is about to find out. He also delves into a very active dreamscape that he can interact with, much like the video games he designs. Mark loves creating his own universe "thread" and exploring connections with others. The only questions are what cannot be designed and what connection cannot be bridged.

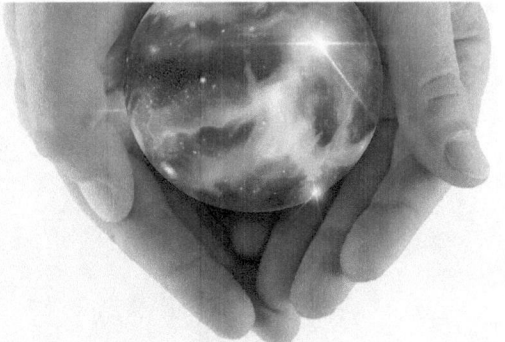

Chapter 1

Moving In

The dark browns mixed with black, while the slivers of red seemingly dance ferociously to an endless depth within as if his eyes are as vast as a galaxy. Mark's smooth skin provides a nice resting place for his trimmed, shimmering auburn hair, which has a shine nearly identical to his eyes. His slightly elongated face has some unique features, which Alice is scrutinizing. His full lips look as if they are made for kissing.

Alice turns and looks at her dresser nearby as she lies in the modern, larger-than-king-size yet soft and silky bed. The picture on top reminds her of how long she has been seeing Mark, with a fond memory of them together beaming back at her. She looks back toward the ceiling. "This is nice," she thought to herself, and it took quantum entanglement to a whole new level.

The patterns on the clean white ceiling are mere garnish for the thoughts meandering through her head. She tries to imagine what it would be like without Mark. He has helped her in a plethora of ways which he probably is not even aware. She grasps her sheets at the thought; her body snuggles with the comfort of the bed and sheets between. Turning again to gaze in Mark's direction, she finds no reason she should allow herself to break from this accord.

Mark had been equally studying Alice's long, shiny black locks of hair and her soft lips. He had difficulty locating a blemish on her skin while admiring her puppy-dog green eyes. Mark's heightened senses tingle with high detail, and his inner satisfaction is replete.

Breaking the beautiful silence, Mark smiles and says, "Amusingly, your bedroom is more familiar to me than mine."

Alice, "At least you like it; I've been trying to improve the Feng Shui.".

A comfortable smile crosses Mark's face. The silk bed is so soft and comfortable, he thinks as he reaches under the sheets toward Alice's back, where he lightly moves his hand, barely touching her skin. Responding with enthusiasm, Alice's lips reach for his, and they begin the exploration of each other's faces.

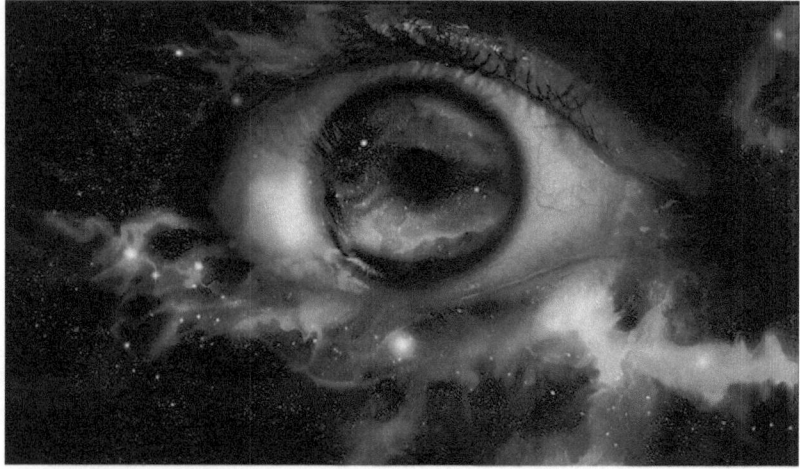

A loud sound interrupts the scene, and Mark swiftly opens his eyes. He stares at the usual ceiling while reaching for his tablet to end the audible alarm.

"Just when it was getting good...damn alarm," he mutters, referring to the vivid, lucid dreams he regularly experiences.

Freeing himself from his silk sheets, he reaches for the piles of clothing not too far from his bed. Stretching back, he effortlessly tosses his throw blanket in a single toss on his bed, causing his bed to look like it is already made with neatly curved folds.

The bare white walls complement the fresh carpet smell of the room he had slept in. Mark has barely begun moving into his newly acquired house, having signed the loan just a few days ago. The clean, sparsely furnished house exuded an exciting vibe of future thrills, where every detail could nearly tell its own story, much like his current life. This house is full of possibilities, he knew would be remarkable. Mark whisks down the stairs while the soft, velvety black carpet shimmers, satisfying his feet; he makes his way to the brand-new kitchen.

With partial attention, Mark casually carves one espresso scoop from the bag and starts his morning cup. Navigating the maze of yet-to-be-unpacked house items, Mark walks to his large exterior deck window. Briefly glancing at his yard, he notices it is a little rough, sparse, and prickly, despite being nicely trimmed.

"One of these days... " Mark says to himself.

Immediately, the TV began displaying the current video news from various Internet sources. The system is preprogrammed to display news on specific topics and items found in the specified news sources.

Mark's mini-tablet suddenly notifies him of an incoming call. The video call opens to what appears to be a view from the sky; the large lake below is approaching at a high velocity. The air blows rapidly, and suddenly, a scream of joy.

"What sizzles, chizzle?" The high-pitched under-duress voice reveals that she is either flying or falling.

"Tina? To what end is the sky falling? I hope that isn't my house at the end of that drop." Mark chuckles.

"Who else would send you a video while bungee jumping? Mairis and I had to rub it in a bit. See ya!"

Tina disconnects, leaving Mark chuckling to himself. "I'll post it to my blog," he thought. This event brought memories flooding his mind about his father taking him to Spirit Rock...

After a long morning hike, Mark, wiping his forehead, marvels at the sweat glistening in the sun as the tiny droplets roll down his hand. The day is warm but not sweltering. His backpack comfortably allows him to keep a perfect posture.

Mark's father, Thekaf, turns and casually brushes the dust from a rock in the shade of a spiring rock formation that had likely existed for millions of years.

He smiles warmly at Mark with a slight laugh, "Remember, son, frequent short breaks and plenty of hydration enable endurance."

Pulling out a bottle of water, Mark hands it to his father, who grips it with his lightly toned, wrinkled, immaculate-looking hands. If it wasn't for a small scar, one might think that Thekaf infrequently worked with his hands.

Admiring the scenery, Mark comments, "The horizon looks surreal, doesn't it?"

He refers to the steep drop cliffs leading to lush green valleys below. Jetting rocks rise high, even above where they are standing.

Thekaf continues, "You'll be setting up camp since it is a useful skill, and I want to ensure you know how it's done."

Mark, "Can I ask questions to make sure I get it right?"

Still smiling, Thekaf's show contemplation, "Of course, son. Is this fun for you?"

"Right now, it's a lot of walking, but I actually really like it," Mark responds matter-of-factly.

"I promise we'll spend more time together."

Less than two hours later, Mark is poised to leap off a very high ledge with gliding wings attached to his back. Mark, strapped into the glider, peers over the cliff's edge. His heart races out of anticipation, and he breathes a long, calming breath. He remembers his father so reassuringly standing right behind him. At that moment, he pushed off the edge and soared through the sky. The fantastic sensation with a touch of nervousness up to the moment, and relief of hitting the ground. It was a little rough, but nothing he couldn't handle himself.

"Hey, bud, you made it! That was a great landing… for a novice. You'll be the maestro of flight in no time!" Mark's father exclaims with a beaming smile and a tiny tear in his eye.

Back to the present, Mark's attention turns to starting his day.

The news shows images of a messed-up room at Dacian's house.

"Intruders ransacked the house of Dacian Wilson. Dacian, a blind resident, typically records the audio of his house, and the trespassers were silent, leaving almost no trace on the audio recordings, suggesting they were aware of the recording system. It took police several hours to detect the activity of the drawers opening, during which they stole personal articles. Puzzling investigators, the apparent intruders stole only a few personal items yet left the house ransacked." The newscast continues, eventually moving to the next story. The TV muffles into the background as Mark makes his way to the shower.

After a quick wash, Mark meticulously details his face, hair, and teeth before quickly tossing a neatly pressed shirt around his torso. He reaches down and swiftly presses his feet into a pair of thin leather slip-on shoes that snugly attach to his feet like a second skin to his ankles. Grabbing his car keys, he makes an exit for his old yet gleaming green Acura TLX.

Shifting into gear, Mark felt exceptionally comfortable in this car. He streams down the small highway with extremely swift maneuvering, causing more than a few slight thrusting movements.

Slowing not nearly enough, Mark turns into the large circular driveway of his father's mausoleum.

Thekaf's retirement fund purchased the private property and mausoleum, the remainder of which is now in a special investment account owned by Mark. Several pictures, flowers, candles, and incense are on a little stand in the middle of the all-stone mausoleum.

Mark approaches the shrine, holding a candle in his hand. Stopping, he places the candle next to the picture and then lights it. Mark looks at the image of his father from a camping trip, recalling memories of the trip—the light from the flame flickers, dancing as if emitting a code of sorts.

Immediately next to the shrine is a high-quality coffin. Mark softly opens the coffin and stands lightly, resting on the coffin. Inside the casket is a peaceful Thekaf beneath a glass cover.

Mark, lightly tearful, speaks to his dead father, "How can we take care of each other now?"

Later that night, Mark reached his bed and shifted off to sleep.

Mark's dream…

Mark looks up from his bed; he is in the same room… his room. Slightly disoriented, he stands up to look around. Suddenly, many giant spiders (some as large as one square foot) gather nearby and around him.

Mark peers closely at one; he can sense the non-human thing that it is. It looks back at him perceptively. Mark looks to the spider's left side, then the right. The spider reacts to Mark's observation by looking in the direction he is looking. The spider lightly rubs one of its right legs when Mark looks to its right. The spider is aware that Mark is looking at it. He slowly bends down and then reaches to touch one sitting on his bed. It was energy, all right. He could feel its texture. The spider lies flat and curls up into a non-threatening stance (playing dead).

The spiders approach and then surround him. They start to move with him like a dance. When he moves, they move. Mark starts walking around his room, and they follow him as he walks.

Suddenly, Mark wakes up in his bed and realizes he was sleeping. He looks at his clock, which reads 1:11 a.m. Mark looks around the room but cannot see the spiders. He rolls over, buries himself into his pillow, and returns to sleep, where he dreams a new dream.

The unstable, slightly shifting, and unclear imagery suggests either interference or a very distant transmission. Despite that, it's a beautiful day on an attractive lake beach stretching for miles, and Thekaf sits in a lounge chair. Behind him are some evergreen pine trees, among other foliage. Dressed for warm weather, Thekaf lounges in shorts and sunglasses.

"Hey, little man, is that you?"

Mark was shocked, "You live?!"

"No need to worry about me; I'm on a pleasant place called Earth."

Akutra-Ramses Atenosis Cea

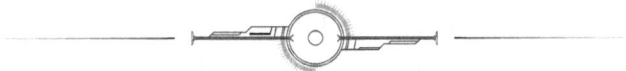

Earlier that morning, Ramses had an unusually early visitor. Opening the enormous doors reveals an all-black figure, which causes the visitor's white eyes to look that much brighter. Luminating the walkway before dawn, several soft yellow lights allowed one to observe the fountain in the distance. Ramses smiles at the sight of his visitor.

"What's the find?"

The black, stealthily clothed person adjusts his spandex facemask before responding. "Not much, merely the subtleties of the ghost within. That said, I may have what you need to send a sociable reply."

He reaches into a black satchel and reveals a manila envelope, then continues, "The optical disc has all the video, and the written report has the rest; all copies are on the disc."

Ramses slips a roll of credits into the masked figure's hand as they exchange the envelope, then concludes the conversation. "You understand that you know nothing about these supposed events on this night, nor Dacian."

The man in black stares at Ramses like the statement was all too obvious, "Uh, yeah… Be sure to arm your alarm, maybe even get a new one, a better one."

"Is there something I should know?"

"Hopefully not, but take care anyway."

Closing the door, Ramses briskly makes for his laptop. Now, to assemble a complete profile, he thought to himself.

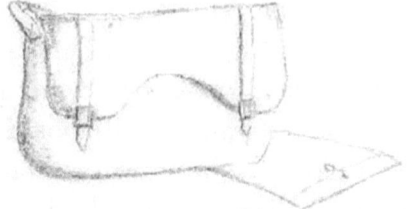

Swiftly browsing the disc, Ramses sighs and then reaches for his mango juice splashed with a bit of vodka.

The disc elaborates on the details surrounding the events, and he was correct; there isn't much found. Slowly sipping his drink, Ramses firmly grasps his forehead and then gives a slight tremble.

Thinking to himself, it is imperative that he locate a clue that might lead to the discovery of what has happened to Selene. Perhaps there is a lead or connection on the disc somewhere. Was she dead? It isn't easy to fathom her simply leaving without notice.

Ramses couldn't help but remember that smile, those eyes, and the laugh. Selene has eyes just like her father. It took him back to her 9th birthday, the bright-eyed excitement. Fulfilled expectations were etched on her face, and the joy in her voice moments before she sprinted toward her awaiting girlfriends. She hadn't yet reached those teenage years in that particular memory. Ramses prefers to remember the moments of happiness, and all other difficulties seem so meaningless now.

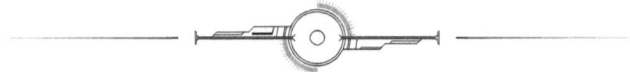

Mark is at his contractor's office. Mark's desk sits in front of his computer in his clean, multi-occupant office, void of any personal effects other than the items he brought. This is his office at Dimensional Storm, and many references to the company are littered around the office and walls. Mark enjoys this job even though the contract is coming to a close.

Sitting at his desk, Mark skillfully manipulates his pointer, maneuvering the on-screen 3-D wireframe to various angles. The design aspect of this job is nearly complete, and he will soon need to find another contract. For now, he continues his task at hand. To Mark's right sits Tink, a slender, lanky male in basic jeans and a T-shirt. Tink shifts back and forth while utilizing the mouse and jotting something on a tablet. His long, dark-brown hair flows around as he repeatedly brushes it out of the way.

"Hey, Tink?" Mark finally says with a smirk.

"Whazzup?... I'm reviewing the Pacific Northwest," Tink responds.

Mark rolls over to Tink's desk and peers at the computer screen. Tink moves through the high-detail rendering of scenery and along a minor road and walkway called Deschutes Parkway, around "Capital Lake." Across the water, a large dome can be seen extending above the trees —a scene from Olympia, WA, USA. It is a place neither of them has ever been to, but Mark designed it in his video game map.

Tink points toward the Capitol dome, "I like that building. It's unique. It's monumental. You should move some of the trees so it can be seen from this nice park."

Mark zaps, "It's a government building. The yard of which takes an honorable mention."

"What's in the yard? You called this city Olympia? It is quite plush and detailed and should be a blast for the players."

"Yeah... " Mark recalls his dreams about his father, "Have you ever heard of a place called Earth? I googled it, but no dice."

"Earth? I... don't think so. Why?"

"My father might be there, so it is my new quest."

Tink finally turns toward Mark with a slightly puzzled look. He is unsure where Mark is going with this.

"Call your father up or someone who knows him."

Mark, slightly sarcastic, "Well, my father is dead, so... "

"Wait, Dad's dead, and you somehow think he is in a place called Earth?"

"Yeah, seems crazy, but I saw him in a dream."

A look of concern comes over Tink. Mark can't be seriously relying on his dreams over the cold, hard facts?

"Wow, so you believe that was really your father and not just a dream?"

Mark emotionally composes himself, holding back teary eyes. Tink obviously doesn't understand, so Mark tries to act casually.

"You don't understand. I must find him."

"Mark, if you need mental help. There is absolutely nothing wrong with that. Several good psychologists in town can help you decipher your dreams. In your dreams, you're probably just trying to cope with his death mentally."

"Please, just look for any references to a place called Earth."

Tink sighs, "I'll see what I can find."

Mark rolls back to his desk, and they both return to work.

Over the intercom, the receptionist announces a visitor, "Mark, you have a visitor. Mairis Tefnut is here in the lobby. Should I send her in?"

Mark responds to the receptionist, "Yes, yes. Send her in!"

He quickly loads his front camera app on his tablet and checks his hair.

Tink responds, looking at Mark, "And she shows up at the office."

Mark gleams, "Yeeah."

Mairis steps into the office area. She is reasonably tall with smooth-flowing curves teasingly but modestly exposed by her relaxed white top and pastel-green skirt that didn't quite reach her knees. She notices Mark and flashes a flirty smirk.

"Hey, Mark!"

"Mairis, what brings you to this part of the galaxy?"

"I just wanted to see your office for myself."

"Uhh, sure. This is it. My home office is more interesting technology-wise."

"Hey, can you give me the tour? I've always wanted to see a place like this."

Mark is suddenly more comfortable showing the operation than his desk, "Yeah. Let me show you around a bit."

They walk around the large corporate office with Mark advising Mairis of each desk and job description. The offices are a mix of open and private spaces with large glass walls.

Eventually, they come upon a large glassed-off room with a couch in the middle. Two males sit on the sofa in extremely casual clothing with blue jeans, colorful anime t-shirts, and baseball caps. Mairis steps inside.

Mark follows, "This is the video game testing room, and these guys are playing one of our games right now."

The game testers are highly animated; occasionally, they rapidly press the buttons and make various simple remarks.

One of the testers takes a slurp of a gigantic 32-ounce energy drink can called Tau and screams, "Yes!" While the other tester grabs some popcorn from a large bowl of popcorn.

Mairis, observing the gameplay, interrupts, "What are you trying to do?"

The playing gamer responds, "Uh, well, in this game, we are on the outskirts of the city of Olympia. A region called Black Lake. What I need to do is airdrop supplies to the protected area right next to the park dock."

"You're trying to drop to that spot on the map? Next to the little beach with all the boats?"

Gamer, "Yeah."

Mark chuckles at Mairis's intensity, thoroughly enjoying the moment.

Mairis starts directing him, "Slightly left... Slightly right... Can you go up just a bit? Wait... wait... Drop now!"

The gamer goes ahead and follows her directions, finally pressing the drop button as specified. The game alerts the supply landing and reports a perfect score.

"Wow, how did you do that? I've been doing this all day and never had a perfect score."

Mairis has a victorious chuckle, "Well, it's basic physics. The game is pretty realistic; I like it."

Mark takes the comment on game realism as a compliment since he designed a lot of the landscape, but also recognizes other team member contributions, "Thanks!... the engine dynamics guys are pretty good."

Chapter 2

Blast from the Past

Ramses yard is well cared for with finely trimmed grass and shrubbery. Extruding from the house into the backyard is a large concrete patio with several chairs and quality-crafted outdoor furniture. Ramses' enormous black BBQ is sizzling with the lid open while resting on its concrete slab adjacent to the patio. Ramses stands at the BBQ in well-pressed, tan-colored shorts complimenting his solid light blue t-shirt. He is tending to various types of meat, chili peppers, and vegetables. There are around thirty people present, all of whom are socializing around the patio and furniture.

Tina suddenly notices Mark's presence and screams, "Mark! You made it!"

Tina is ready for the weather in leggings and a loose-fitting summer top covering a bikini. Tina's silky blond hair is clearly well cared for, with bangs lightly and purposely hanging over her forehead. She rushes to Mark, who is now near Ramses at the BBQ.

Mark acknowledges her, "Tina, whazzup! Nice place for a BBQ."

She is excited that the BBQ has finally started; Tina briefly moves the hair out of her face.

As if presenting the scene, she motions around and says, "Yeah, Ramses is 'fully equipped.'"

Ramses divides his attention between the barbequing peppers and Mark's presence. He doesn't look up but says, "Mark! Now we can paint the town red."

Settling down, Tina stands casually holding some unknown beverage in her right hand as she plots for an icebreaker, "How do you like Olympus?"

"It has its good points," Mark states with positivity.

"I was born and raised here, so I know all the secret cool kid hangouts," Tina sips her beverage and pauses, observing how comfortable Mark and Ramses stand next to each other before continuing, "In fact, Mark, I helped Thekaf locate some unique spots."

Mildly surprised, Mark reacts, "You knew my father? I'll most certainly call you on that."

She casually looks Mark over, observes his reaction, and smiles. She knows she struck gold with that reference.

Ramses looks up from the grilling spread, "I personally can do without the grimy ghetto of Memphra."

"Yeah, I liked Memphra, but Olympus doesn't seem to have a ghetto. Even the poorer areas are cleaner."

Slightly animated with her finger while holding her beverage, Tina's eyes meander between Mark and Ramses, "You know... I'm working on my skydiving instructor's license, so if you guys ever want to go skydiving, I'm your girl."

Mark responds well to his new local friend, "I'll certainly take you up on that."

Ramses wipes the sweat from his brow as he reacts to Tina's multiple 'offers' to hang out. "Tina, you're fun just the way you are."

Shifting and leaning against a short stone wall separating the BBQ patio and the grassy yard, Mark looks distantly in contemplation, "I recall many BBQs at your Memphra apartment."

Sipping a beer, Ramses turns toward Mark, "Yeah, the patio was smaller, but the view was excellent."

Mark re-joins Ramses' cheerful nature, "Remember when Daniel threw the plant over the rail?"

Surprised by the revelation into the party life, Tina stammers, "Seriously?"

Ramses continues, "He actually thought he could do anything he wanted, including that."

Tina queries, "Including the pot?"

"Yes, the ceramic pot as well. It was quite a shock for people on the ground floor."

Still with her jaw slightly dropped, Tina exclaims, "Wwow!"

Mark softly reaches over and grips Ramses' shoulder, then whispers, "You seem fine... but I know that missing a daughter is a pain few can understand."

In response, Ramses struggles to maintain his composure, "Yeah."

Mark barely above a whisper, "We'll find her. I'll do whatever it takes."

"Thanks, Mark."

Satisfied with the progress of the sizzling food, Ramses closes the BBQ lid and places his tongs down. Turning toward his visitors, he waves his hand.

"Good evening, all! I hope you're having a good time."

A jovial Rae interrupts, "A toast! Too many good years ahead, and to my good friend Ramses!"

Everyone lifts their glass, and some announce, "Here! Here!"

"Thank you, Rae." Ramses pauses briefly to allow his guests to finalize the toast, then continues, "As many of you know, I called this BBQ in honor of my now-missing daughter, Selene. The exact timing of her disappearance is unknown, but she has been missing for several days now. If anyone gains any knowledge of her whereabouts, please let me know as soon as possible."

Several guests mumble about the announcement.

Surprised, Rae announces, "I assume you've reported her status to the police?"

Mark takes the opportunity to ask a question he has been meaning to ask, "Do you have any details about her disappearance?"

"Yes, yes. I have reported her missing, and they are looking into it. Isn't that right, Thoth?"

Thoth lifts his glass assuredly, "Absolutely, we'll find her."

"Now, please… enjoy this exquisite evening; the food will be ready shortly."

Ramses turns toward Mark in a low tone, "I have some additional information and would appreciate it if you could review it."

Mark whispers back, "Sure thing."

Ramses continues in a low tone, "Hey, Mark? Have any good dreams lately?"

Mark lifts his beverage with a smile, "Always."

Ramses continues, "I know you explore, but I felt it would be good for you to physically get out a little."

Mark jabs a response, "A BBQ is good for that, but rest assured, I get out when possible."

Tina interrupts. "Ramses, my day job is at police HQ, so I'll be sure to remind them to do everything they can to find Selene."

"Thank you, Tina."

SpiderSilk

    Mark is sitting at the oversized desk, which is littered with large monitors and a computer setup advanced enough to have a personal cloud rack system in his home office. On the desk is an open manila envelope labeled Selene.

    Most monitors have remote desktop windows open and live feeds from around his house and work. Mark has his portable wireless micro-disk reader on the side. Mark intently looks at one of the screens, playing a video from the tiny disc given to him by Ramses.

    The playing video is a surveillance video from one of the last places Selene was seen, a fully automated car charging station.

    After a moment, Mark drinks from his bottled water while sitting back in his chair, still casually watching the video, when Selene drives into the camera view.

    "There she is."

    Mark sits forward to get a better view. Selene pulls up in her little sports car and exits the driver's seat. She plugs her vehicle in and suddenly looks at the maintenance building nearby. There is no audio, but it is obvious she is talking.

    Selene walks toward the building and starts what appears to be intensely screaming. Mark cannot see anything in the direction of her screams. Selene pulls out a small spray bottle and sprays it at a dark corner of the building. She then turns and frantically disconnects the charger and leaves.

Mark zooms in and watches the scene again. The video is a little grainy, but Selene appears to be spraying pepper spray. Additionally, there is nothing except the wall where she is spraying. Mark does notice the wall and ground had black, dark coloring as though someone had lightly sprayed them with spray paint.

He zooms in. Close up, he can tell it isn't just a shadow; it is colored black. Mark sits back in the chair, takes another drink of water, and then sighs.

Mark's dream later that night.

Mark approaches his father's large stone mausoleum. He looks around the stone structure, but there is nothing out of the ordinary. Mark walks around to the back of the structure; there is no path, but the finely trimmed lawn edges up to the small concrete foundation slabs.

He reaches the back of the mausoleum, where he sees a door similar to a cellar door. Opening the door reveals another standard door below a set of descending stairs. Mark steps down the stairway and grips the door handle, opening the door.

To Mark's surprise, inside is a library of old, authentic books, scrolls, and several computers rather than the expected mausoleum storage. Mark walks around the room and then sits at one of the computers. The dust-free desk is neat and minimal; the chair is a comfortable rolling chair, nothing fancy.

Reaching for the mouse, he notices an old, worn scroll beside him. Shifting, he picks up the scroll and then opens it. The scroll appears to be a star chart with several stars and even planets, but only one star system stands out. It is labeled Ard. Mark quickly looks at all the stars nearby (Siryus, Qinturus, Mamajek, etc.) and repeats the names to himself to help with memory.

Mark returns to the computer and presses some keys on the loud, mechanical grey keyboard. The screensaver vanishes. The computer is already logged in and has a picture of the scroll he had just reviewed. He can see that the label gives it a name, the Tarran scroll.

Mark looks inside the computer folder where the file is located. Several other items are inside, pictures of artifacts, but no other star charts. The artifacts are labeled "Ard" items (i.e., Ard digital disk artifact #1995).

Getting up from the chair, Mark walks out of the mausoleum storage. He starts running down the street, and the scenery shifts quickly, blending.

Mark awakens to a deep growl. He swiftly sits up. His room is extremely dark, even with his eyes already adjusted. Another louder growl comes from an unlit part of the room.

Mark jumps up and reaches a recently unpacked small desk near his bed. On the desk is a small desk lamp.

He turns on the light and loudly says, "Is there something in the dark?"

Mark walks carefully toward the direction from which the noise seems to have come. Examining the dimly lit area, there is nothing to be seen.

He returns to his bed, leaving the small light on; he then drifts off to another dream.

Mark's Dream, a small city North of Olympus.

Mark is crouching behind the side wall of a home décor shop. In his right hand is the water balloon. Next to him, rubbing up against him, is Alice, also crouching. Alice has a bottle of vegetable oil in her left hand. She is peering around the corner where she can see inside the shop.

After a moment, Alice turns to Mark.

Alice, "Okay, let's go!"

They quietly sneak into the shop. Alice slowly opens the door, trying to avoid the doorbell announcement, as Mark slips in. Looking towards the back of the shop, Mark notices product displays while he quietly creeps forward. Near the back of the store, there is a large quantity of dark, mystical décor, including tools for setting up shrines and rituals, complete with guns and large knives.

Very slowly, Alice closes the door while the shopkeeper places some stock on the shelves on the other side of the shop. Mark approaches the shopkeeper while Alice quietly walks up behind him.

Immediately behind the shopkeeper, Alice pours all the oil onto the shop floor. She fights to keep from laughing or making any noise at all. After sufficient oil has flooded the floor, Mark says, "Are you the owner of this establishment?"

The shopkeeper jolts out of shock at their presence.

He says, "How did you sneak up on me like that?"

Mark zaps back, "I do apologize."

After a sigh, he answers, "Yes, yes. This is my shop."

Alice tries to hold back a laugh about what is about to happen, "Wow, you even work in your dreams?"

A matter-of-fact response comes from the shopkeeper, "Sometimes it feels like it."

Alice whispers, "He doesn't know it's a dream." She grabs an artesian bowl off the shelf and quickly runs toward the door. Mark is right behind her.

The shopkeeper quickly responds, "Hey, don't take that!"

He steps down onto the oily floor and then proceeds to chase them. He immediately loses footing. Flapping around in the oil, the shopkeeper grunts, trying to regain himself in the slippery oil.

Mark hurls the water balloon at the shopkeeper's groin, "Wet dreams, knucklehead!"

The balloon successfully lands and bursts, soaking the shopkeeper's pants and groin. Mark turns and runs just behind Alice. They swiftly exit the shop and keep running, where Alice starts laughing. Shortly after they are some distance from the shop, they stop for a second to catch their breath.

Alice is breathing hard, "His sheets are gonna' need a wash!"

They both laugh.

Suddenly, the shopkeeper comes out of the shop with his soaked pants and starts running after them.

Alice looks at Mark in surprise, "Oops!"

They turn to run when the man suddenly vanishes.

Mark, full of smiles, "Let me guess; he woke up. His shop is still here?"

Alice responds, "Yeah, lucky for us, his mind still maintains it."

Mark nodded, quickly offering an alternative answer, "Or it's a permanent imprint."

They catch their breath and then return to the shop. The door is unlocked, and the shopkeeper is no longer anywhere to be seen. They carefully look around in case the shopkeeper returns. Mark can't help but notice how neat and clean everything is. Tina reaches for the front door and turns the "open" sign to "closed" while Mark looks for the back-office door.

A short way behind the register are multiple doors, one to the bathroom and one to the back office. Mark checks the office door, and it is unlocked. Motioning to Tina, he opens the door and enters the small, dimly lit office.

The office looked like it came out of the '50s or '60s. The plain room with a concrete floor has one small, dust-free desk. Around the walls are various boxes of what is likely spare inventory. At the desk is a dimly lit, yellow, warm lamp, some old-looking pens, and an ancient rotary phone. At the desk is a simple padded office chair.

Mark grabs the chair and sits at the office desk; the chair makes very little noise as it scrapes across the concrete due to its unworn rubber pads. Everything is of sturdy yet simple construction. He sifts through the desk and opens the drawers. The desk drawer on the side opens to several filing cabinet folders.

Mark turns and notices Tina just behind, "Wow, paper. A computer would have been more secure in this place."

Tina replies, "Yeah. He probably mistakenly thinks it is more secure."

Mark sifts through the folders and finds one marked "Sales Slips." Pulling the folder, Mark examines the slips for names and addresses.

Smiling, Mark says, "Help me look for addresses in Olympus."

Alice replies, "Give me a stack."

The next morning, Mark is sitting at his home computer. He stares at the Google prompt momentarily in thought. Then, using his mouse, he clicks the Celeste button, which takes him to Google Celeste, an online complete celestial body map of known celestial bodies.

He types Ard, but the results are missing the target system he saw in his dream. He types Tarran, but still no results. Again, he inputs Qinturus, and one result shows "al-Qinturus." Mark clicks his only lead. Moments later, a detailed map of the celestial area for Alpha Centauri A.

"Yes!"

Mark zooms out a bit, and sure enough, there is Ard, Mamajek, and a little further to the right is Siryus, except Siryus is called Sopdet. Ard is not named. Mark clicks on it, but Google says it is an unknown system. He zooms in on a distant, fuzzy picture of our solar system, which features eight planets, including Earth. From this view, Pluto is obscured by the Kuiper belt. Mark pauses to look at the solar system to see if he recognizes anything. There are no names on the planets.

Mark clicks on each planet, but Google repeatedly says unknown celestial body:

"Dang."

Mark clicks "Save" to ensure he keeps the find.

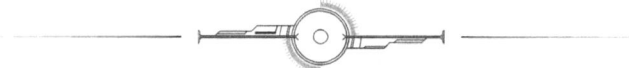

"Tink, will you 'show' at my housewarming party?"

Tink, showing genuine interest, swiftly turns to look him in the eye. "Dress code? No jeans, then? How much of the dress code and 'reality,' for that matter, is interpretable?" Tink's dark eyes and long hair made him look like he could be Indian.

"You can either be in costume or nice attire. Yeah, people have various ideas on what 'code' is; it's for the picture, you know what I mean? It should look the part. I want to learn as well as write a bit." Mark zapped.

"I'll be there like an apparition," Tink responded assuredly, with absoluteness.

After a full day of work and organizing the house, Mark finally located his bed and shifted into a state of sleep.

Mark's dream later that night.

Mark finds himself traveling along a mainland beach populated with palm trees. Looking inland, he pushes upward, immediately leaping high into the crisp, starry night air. He begins to soar a great distance, and he has complete control over direction, which is common in his dreams. Despite frequently having control, Mark still enjoys soaring around, and with a beaming smile, he pushes left, then right.

Mark screams with joy, "Yeah!"

As he begins to descend, he pushes upward again and leaps even without land underfoot. After traveling for some time, he comes upon a small town. Here, he descends in a controlled manner and lands with a hard thump, causing the ground to shake a bit.

Mark stands up and begins walking through the dimly lit town, which looks like it could be somewhere in Colorado. A few streets down, a sense of unease seems to be building as if some danger is lurking. Mark decides to investigate and comes upon a dark figure or creature; he cannot discern its exact form.

Mark opens his hand, and in his palm, a large luminous question mark appears. The figure turned, its beady little yellow eyes looking his way and slowly circling him. Suddenly, it dashed his way. Right behind it, another person knelt, and a wave of gravel sprayed toward the feet of the approaching creature.

In the distance, there are two men in long flowing robes. They step on the corners of what appeared to be a large, bright-blue padded mat. Standing, each of them lift their shoulders, causing the robes to drop to the mat quickly. With swift-moving limbs, they stand in a martial arts defensive stance, obviously preparing to fight each other.

Mark swiftly focuses his eyes, which become so hot that they emit a thick, luminous, forceful wave. The creature, suddenly exposed to the light, is caught off guard. It hesitates out of shock and stumbles from the wave, grasping at where it is hit. At that moment, the wave of gravel pelted its feet, causing the creature to lose balance and fall backward on its backside.

The dark figure speaks, "You seers are all the same."

Very quickly, it jolts up and makes for the hills in the distance. A crow, sitting on a nearby tree branch, immediately makes flight in the same direction.

Mark looks at the other boy and smirks as they high-five. Fireworks illuminate the background as they conduct a victory handshake. Garrick is someone whom Mark seems to meet frequently, but only in these very real, lucid dreams. He has come to recognize him as a worthy ally and collaborator.

Garrick says, "We meet again."

Mark responds positively, "Yeah, I lost count! Another day, another adventure. Thanks for helping with that."

Garrick's smile turns to a mildly pleasant facial expression, "Anytime. Any idea what he meant about seers?"

Mark replies, "I could see him if that's what he meant."

They lightly laugh.

Suddenly, Mark opens his eyes to his plain white-walled room.

Chapter 3

Tragic Leap

Several years ago, on a distant planet located a few light-years away from a black hole in a completely different galaxy. A story of an encounter with an anomaly unfolds...

An overweight and blind security guard with extremely short blond hair lightly overfills the reasonably nice black office chair that appears to be struggling to contain the man. He sits behind a long desk merged with computer control panels, all of which are attached to the wall just under the immense windowed view. The sizeable tinted glass panels reveal a forest view on a sunny day. The sun sporadically blasts through the very tall beech trees, providing a natural cover for the observable forest floor.

The security guard is relaxed, fidgeting a little out of boredom in the quiet yet large room. There is minimal noise coming from the computers that are hidden from sight and the occasional movement of the guard's lightly squeaky chair in the otherwise quiet room. He leans forward and presses a button. One of the many buttons that have brightly painted raised dots in a language we know as braille.

The computer announces, "High-pressure zone continues to dominate the area with subsiding air for a light, breezy eight mph wind."

In walks another blind, slender security guard carrying two coffees and a paper bag. Setting the coffee down next to the two unused earpieces known as range scanners, he feels around the bag and removes a footlong sub, then hands it to the guard still sitting in his chair.

"Ever thin' A-O-K, Ivan?"

Ivan, the overweight guard, responds, "Another beautiful day."

The slender guard sets one coffee near Ivan and then sits in the nearby vacant office chair with the other coffee. Ivan prepares his sub for consumption.

Taking a bite of the sub, Ivan reaches forward and presses another button on one of the panels.

The computer announces, "For sector 10 o'clock of 90 degrees: Activity 40%, maximum thermal size objects 7.1 Square feet, no bipedal pack movement detected, non-thermal movement 1%, no detected organized non-thermal movement."

The slender guard, Dimitri, comments, "Same as yesterday 'bout this time."

Ivan sighs and softly laughs at the non-eventful nature of the job, then takes another bite of his sub. Suddenly, the computer starts making a lot of clicking noises. The overweight guard curiously listens before dropping his sub. He reaches forward and reads the dynamic braille screens that would shift with updates as he reads them with his thick, lightly greasy fingers.

The computer announces, "Unusual activity detected for sector 9 o'clock of 50 degrees."

Dimitri, "What's the screen say?"

Ivan barks at Dimitri, "That can't be right... Run the Muon imager."

Dimitri reaches for the computer panel, turns one of the dials to 9 o'clock, and then presses a button.

"The muon imager says there's water, a lot of it."

"The density is correct for a body of water... that makes no sense. You recall the sensor check I just ran a few minutes ago?"

Dimitri nods in agreement., "Computer, run diagnostics."

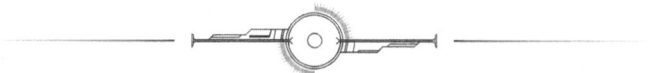

Chris holds the recorder to his mouth and says, "Today was a good day. Financial numbers are up, quality numbers are up, and costs are down. The new 'Explorer IV' power tool is selling nicely; now we have to ensure that the 'Explorer V' can top it. I must discuss it with our technology investors." Releasing the record button, he pondered his approaching plans.

"Damn—Those technology investors. I would be very rich right now if they did not have me one over," Thoughts linger in his mind.

"Perhaps my plans are too docile?" He continues to himself while reflecting on the liquid in his beverage cup.

Pressing the recording button again, "Seek ways to automate any and all technology-provisioned processes or components."

"If I can maneuver on top of this, I may be able to reduce my dependence on those expensive yet necessary technologists. What would it be like to go without technology?" That question made him cringe, "It may be a necessary evil, but I can still eliminate as many of those bastards as possible."

A raspy, disembodied voice speaks from the darkness, "Don't worry about technologists... You are the selected one; you will help us take Olympus."

Chris does not appear to hear the voice, yet responds to it immediately.

Pressing the recording button again, he continues, "On second thought, don't over-focus on removing the technology dependency."

Chris's office is a modest 100 square feet with a wooden desk against the back wall. The computer interface is the basic braille keyboard, but it could interface directly to his range scanner earpiece, making it easier than ever to use. Chris, however, really liked his thin mesh flexible rolling chair.

Suddenly, his senses tingle, and he notices an approaching person. It is Dacian. Chris could tell by the various manners of movement and noise he was sensing. Dacian's heavy thrusting actions and slightly brutish meander were easily recognizable, especially to Chris, who had known him for quite some time. Chris reaches for his 'range scanner' and places it in his ear. This fantastic new version can even detect light and allows the user to graphically 'see' a matrix display with the ear. Dacian has just opened the slightly oversized wooden door.

"Hello, Chris! How is it?" The slightly thick person standing just inside the doorway is a friend and technical advisor of Chris's.

Chris faces Dacian and responds, "Well, you know. Numbers are up, and costs are down, so pretty well."

The odor of Dacian is fresh, and he had obviously recently showered. "Are your technology guys still 'raykin' most of the credits?"

Dacian laughs; he has discussed this with Chris on numerous occasions. Chris chuckles with him at his response, which implies a 'yes.'

"There is more to life than technology, despite the tech-rabid nature of our society!" Dacian chuckles.

Dacian sighs with a positive tone.

"Listen, I need to discuss something with you that came up on one of our exploration radar sensors, and it's not about technology. No rush. Can we schedule something for tomorrow? Say, 10?"

"Does it have anything to do with massive beams of light in the sky detected by our new light scanners?" Astronomers were making discoveries daily about what lies beyond the planet.

"No, it is actually here on the planet."

Chris smiles to himself, which Dacian can probably detect.

"Yes, that sounds great! It's been a while anyway, and we could catch up. Meet me here, and we'll breeze over to the Waverider for brunch and coffee or something."

Dacian turns toward the exit. "I'll be there. Talk to you later!"

39

Feeling around, Chris locates his secure access device, jacket, and walking stick. Swiftly rising, Chris makes for the exterior where his 'traveler' is stationed. Chris recalls his grandfather rambling on about what early versions of the travelers were like. He laughs at that; how primitive life must have been.

Approaching his front door, Chris's range scanner advises him that it is unlocked and is opening as the sensor is programmed to do upon detecting Chris. A nice fresh scent is in the air, yet Chris can detect some pattern forming that may be less pleasant. Briskly stepping inside, Chris can sense the smell and form of his slender companion, Ekaa.

"Heelloo! How was your day?" Chris cheerfully sounded.

Turning toward Chris, Ekaa responds with an unsteady tone. "Just incredulous now that you are here!"

Chris responds in kind. "Is there anything else? Is there something wrong?"

Ekaa softly grabs Chris's hand and then leads him to sit down.

"It's Darven. He is so smart and has been achieving good enough grades to go to a really nice university. I was thinking of trying to get him into Boxington Wave. I know it's a bit far away, but it is for the best."

Chris contemplates that briefly, then responds. "That is one of the more expensive schools and will be difficult to afford with everything else going on."

Ekaa whines and mumbles a bit. "I KNOW! It's tha-that I want to enable him to attain a good future. Better than we have if possible."

Chris reaches for his mouth and softly rubs it while considering his financials. "Darn, if those—damned— technology investors didn't take so many credits. I mean—the company is doing well right now, but it'll take time to attain the extra funds."

Ekaa mumbles a bit again. "I don't think Darven has time. Really standard grades complete in one year at the most two, and he will need to start within a year, or he'll get a slow start in life. You know how that goes, kids who get a slow start!?"

Chris turns and fiddles with his lips. "Hmmm--- yes, a slow start means less time, fewer opportunities, and can be more difficult. I'll try to think of something."

Ekaa then responds with positivity. "Well, let's eat dinner and sound graph a movie. I'm a bit tired and would like to relax into rest period."

Chris smiles and breathes sharply. "That is a great idea for an ending to this day."

Standing up, Chris walks into the living area where his daughter Lada sits. She has taken over the area with crayons and pictures spread out on the long wooden coffee table, as well as part of the floor. Lada, crayon in hand, is sitting on the edge of the soft, cushioned couch and is leaning over a crayon drawing of an eye. Sporadically humming, she moves to the same beat she is humming.

"What you up to, Booboo?"

Lada looks up, "Daddy!"

Chris sits on the couch next to her, then reaches his arm around her, hugging her while he looks at the crayon art.

"I'm drawing Daddy."

With her free hand, Lada starts playing with the range scanner in her ear.

Chris, showing genuine interest in her drawings, intently scans the colorful creations of Lada, "Oh, yeah?"

Ekaa responds to Lada, fondling the range scanner, "Don't fidget with your scanner, honey; you remember what happened to the last one?"

Lada puts her hand down, then looks at Chris and smiles, "It's an eye! You like it?"

Chris affectionately smiles brightly, "I do, I do. Where did you get the idea to draw an eyeball?"

Lada responds to Chris while looking at Ekaa, "Grandpa said his daddy told him there used to be people who could see with them."

"Those are just stories, Booboo," Chris kisses her on her forehead, "Now come on, let's eat dinner."

Dabbling in his coffee, Chris queries Dacian. "So, what's going on that we need to discuss?"

Dacian sounds excited as he responds. "Well, we have some very odd readings from one of our deep woods' sonars. It's reading all kinds of things that should not be there. We even collaborated with a Romadium team to run scans from the other side of the forest, and guess what?"

Chris is still not sure and replies, "More unusual readings?"

Dacian, still eager, says, "They didn't detect us. In fact, the sensors gave a readout that suggested there was a body of water in the location we should have been detected or liquid of some sort. We need to send in a scouting team."

Chris quickly recognizes where this is going, "Sounds great! When do we go check this out?"

Dacian flags the waiter for more coffee and then responds. "How about tomorrow?!"

Now Chris is interested. "Okay, so let me get this correct. The sensors suddenly started reporting a different landscape?"

Dacian laughs at the bizarre nature of that. "Yes! It's like the detection waves are not getting through or something."

Chris sips his coffee. "Or it is getting readings from far away and somehow confusing them. Interference? I mean, I know our scanners have vastly improved recently, but to give such readings suggests that they are possibly malfunctioning."

Dacian intensifies, "I thought of that. What would be powerful enough to interfere with all our sensors? Even the Romadium sensors? Mind you, these sensors work fine elsewhere."

Chris flags the waiter. "Charge, please."

Dacian, "I'll locate a few people that should go with us on this trip and make shuttle arrangements."

Chris is walking toward the shuttle with John Cords. A light breeze gently nudges clothes and hair on a reasonably sunny day.

"Ever been outside of Braila?" Chris queries his friend John Cords while paying attention to every detail of his bio-patterns.

"Me? No, not ev-aa. All my business has been here until this point. My parents used to travel to the Black Ocean for outings. After we acquired a nice pool, I have been too busy to frolic as such. I can find fun in town and save on transport time," John says, chuckling a bit.

Chris sympathizes with the extra use of time, then responds, "Well, we are about to go to the edge of the state of Vular. Specifically, it is somewhere near the Titu Forest and not far from the border with Romadium."

Akutra-Ramses Atenosis Cea

"This most certainly requires our investigation; what could our scanners be detecting? This could lead to advances in our technology beyond anything we've heard of thus far. It sounds just like what we need: a breakthrough!" John retorts.

"Yeah, I hope it's something interesting. Some people in Romadium think that we might be on the cusp of some amazing natural evolution that will change our technological scenario and needs." Chris thought of John and his blatant endorsement of progress and technology as a sort of poster boy of the previous generation.

Nearly bursting into a laugh, John is apparently not done with his endorsement: "The rise of Man came with his development of advanced tools."

Chris mumbles in a low tone, "What an old man answer."

John, "What was that?"

Chris responds, covering himself, "We have many tools today, yet I wonder what kind of natural evolution we might have without them."

Romadium, on the other hand, has a popular movement towards less technology and more nature. Chris ponders what it might be like to move there. He had heard stories of people who could somehow learn to perceive information 'visually' without the aid of a scanner or even light. That would be a true evolution. If something like that should occur suddenly, everyone would seem at an evolutionary disadvantage, and nature has a way of moving on.

Dacian announces himself as he whisks by, "Time to board the shuttle! You'll like these private shuttles; it is one perk of a VIP agency account."

Swiftly grabbing their gear, Chris and John follow.

"About how long is the flight? Do you know?" John zaps.

Slightly pausing, Dacian responds, "It's a two-hour flight."

Observing the craft, the body is wider than a typical airplane we might use, with several fewer seat rows. At the front, on the wall to the forward cabin, are several three-dimensional art pieces perfect for discovering via touch. The seats are large, wide, brown leather cushioned seats.

"Nice seating, man!" John stammers.

They shortly settle and, without delay, depart the private landing pad.

"Here we go!" Chris toasts a safe and successful trip.

Forty-five minutes into the trip, Chris suddenly hears one of the engines sputtering. "What was that?" Chris swiftly stammers.

Dacian turns toward him and says, "I am sure they are prepared for small contingencies; I'll check with the pilot."

Quickly returning, Dacian sounds assured. "Some debris was stuck in the engine. They restarted it to break it free. They reassured me it was nothing they could not handle. Not to worry, we are still on schedule to 'own' amazing discoveries this trip will bring!"

Dacian is clearly so excited that minor issues like this are like swatting at a fly.

The shuttle resumes smooth flight until suddenly jolting and jerking with force.

"What the heck was that?" John is the first to respond this time.

Dacian is already on it and trying to brace himself as he stumbles toward the flight control area.

After a few moments, he returns. "A freak storm appeared out of nowhere. I mean, it wasn't detected on the radar, and then it was suddenly right in front of us."

Chris is about to say something when a large, crackling electrical noise erupts. Within moments, everything goes quiet except the outside storm.

"Did we lose power?" Chris screams.

"That we did. Brace for impact!" Dacian responds swiftly.

Emerging from flight control, an assistant announces, "Please, remain calm. Brace for impact according to the safety procedure protocol. Air-breathing apparatuses are in the left arm of your seat, and if you need it, the seat cushion will act as a flotation device."

"A flotation device? Is there water!?" Dacien exclaims. Even though they are likely about to crash into an unknown anomaly during a freak anomalous storm, Dacian shows excellent intensity, like a child opening a Christmas present.

"I-I am not sure," Is all that the bewildered flight attendant can muster.

Chapter 4

The Party

Back to Olympus, present day.

After finalizing the placement of his furniture and equipment, Mark's house was finally furnished and ready for the night. Mark sets up the door equipment as the sushi and hors d'oeuvres arrive via his excellent friend Ramses.

"You're up! Are you ready for the approaching boiler?"

Ramses' slightly wavy jet-black hair wisps lightly on his head. His thin dark eyebrows complemented his deep-seated dark-brown eyes and his smooth, permanently tanned skin. His hair was cut very short near the neckline and was progressively longer until the bangs flowed to his forehead. He sports a shiny blue-and-black rayon shirt with a solid brass zipper zipped down just enough to expose a smooth, lightly muscular chest and some gold necklaces.

Mark, still in his silk robe, motions them to enter, "Almost... now that the hors d'oeuvres have arrived, this is going to be huge. I am preparing for a possible atomic reaction."

Mairis jovial, "Hey Mark!"

Mark smiles, "Mairis, nice to see you again!"

SpiderSilk

Mark steps outside to obtain an immediate sensory readout. It is a warm sunny day with birds flapping that can barely be heard in the distance. The air is unusually light and crisp yet feels fresh as the sun's heat warms his skin like the perfection of the day thus far. In the distance, a single lenticular cloud provides an odd sensation. Suddenly, out of the corner of his eye, he notices a ferret. With a flash, it swiftly chases what appears to be a lizard of some sort, possibly a sandstone night lizard.

Mark remarks while alerting Ramses, "How unusually dapper is that?" Ferrets are animals Mark considers quite posh.

Ramses smirks in a playfully lofty manner, "An opulent omen! If I were superstitious, I would only hope that the animal's chase does not refer to some issue ahead."

Tina smiles, fondling and squeezing Ramses, "A good omen indeed!"

Mairis, "I'm not really superstitious, but Ferrets are pretty cool."

Returning inside, Mark closes the door behind them.

Mark laughs at Tina's playfulness. He knows she is not dating Ramses, yet you can hardly tell if it weren't for the lack of kissing.

Ramses, "You smell that?... It's that new house smell. A nice blend of fresh paint and new carpet with a hint of fresh wood and drywall. "

Mark, "Let's hope it remains after the party."

Hanging all around Ramses is Tina. Rubbing his forearm, she leans on him. "We're going to make the Qi of this place pulsate!" Tina zaps.

Tina always likes to show off her friends and how friendly they are. It was a way of portraying that she had a good network.

Mark beams with the excitement of socializing in his fresh house. He pops a can of hard seltzer and then points at the beverage refrigerator, "Beverages are in the frig."

He looks at Mairis, holding back his attraction, "That was hilarious; the look on the video game tester's face was priceless!"

Mairis is pleased with herself, "Games fascinate me; it is a combination of math and creativity."

Tina chimes in while pulling a mineral water from the fridge, "I don't play too many video games, but I suppose I prefer the ones with a world to explore and fun things to do."

Mark, "Games with worlds to explore are like threads in the multiverse."

Mairis, with an exuberant attitude in a slightly lower tone, "One day, I was doing Yoga in the downward dog position, and it dawned on me the creativity of video game world-building."

Tina beams at Mairis' comment, "You'll have to show me how to do yoga like that."

Ramses, "Every video game has a problem for the player to solve, even if it doesn't have realistic physics."

"I suppose that's what gamers like about them," Mairis says in response to Ramses.

Mark looks toward Tina, "I'm glad you're here. I like having you around."

Tina squeezes Ramses' muscles and then recalls that as a little girl, everything seemed so fun, even when life was hard. Growing up, friends were everything, and all too often, they would part ways. Her mind flashed to her childhood best friend, who just slowly seemed to have lost interest in hanging out with her, and how difficult it was for Tina. Since then, she told herself that a strong network will get her everything she needs and wants.

Mark continues about the party, "Right now, I am setting up the badge printer. As they pay the cover charge entrance fee, we will print a custom badge with their signature and name surrounded by the party imagery and slogan."

Ramses smoothly returns, "Ah yes, the Faces of Reality Party, and what exactly is reality?"

Mark laughs again, "Our epic adventure, of course, as it does not require a delusion of the mind."

"Ah, yes, reality... It's of our own creation, so why not own it?" Ramses says with a sly chuckle.

"It's far better than that other place, wherever that is." It was easy to detect Tina's humorous sarcasm.

Suddenly, a sharp pain overcomes Mark's head, and everything becomes blurry.

Ramses is quick to notice, "Hey, Mark? You ok?"

Mark goes limp and falls onto the soft, velvety carpet. Jolting to action, Ramses rushes over to where Mark is. Mark's body is completely limp and lifeless.

Surprised by the events, Tina zaps, "Oh, my god! Check his pulse!"

Ramses squeezes Mark's wrist and then places his finger under his nose.

Ramses, "His pulse is there... He's breathing."

Tina breathes a sigh of relief, "He's alive. Thank the gods! Doesn't look like a seizure... Could he have fainted?"

Mairis suddenly finds herself having trouble breathing, repeatedly gasping for air. She begins to shake slightly as a feeling of weakness comes over her.

Tina looks back at Mairis, "Oh my god, she's having a panic attack... Mairis, honey, concentrate on your breath."

Tina reaches over, hugs Mairis, and directs her to sit down. Mairis, terrified and still gulping breaths, stammers between breaths

"Th-ey are he-re; Th-e're go-ing to take me a-way."

I'm a little surprised, Tina queries, "Who are they? Who is going to take you away?"

Mairis continues stammering, "The- spirits. I don't know who they are!"

Tina slightly shifts her eyes and slowly nods her head, "Nobody's going to take you away; it's just a panic attack."

Ramses lifts Mark's legs in the air. Let's get the blood to his brain. Tina is still trying to calm Mairis down.

She continues, "Breath… there is nothing to worry about; concentrate on your breath."

Ramses checks Mark's eyes by opening his otherwise closed eyelids.

Tina, looking at Mark's eyes, "They look dilated. Mark, please! We love you. Come back to us, but more importantly, I need someone to send crazy videos to!"

Ramses, now feeling uneasy and shaking, is suddenly even more concerned with the situation and yells, "Call emergency services!"

In Mark's unconscious yet dreaming mind, another sort of battle is occurring…

The entire scene has minimal light, with a light outline of Mark on a rough, flat surface, void of anything else. Mark looks around but still cannot see. He shakes his head and blinks his eyes.

Mark stammers out, "Where am I?"

A low, raspy voice comes from the dark void, "You'll find out soon enough."

Mark, "Am I still at my home in Olympus?"

The voice speaks intentionally, undermining Mark, "You're basically a homeless bum at the moment and Olympus… Olympus will be ours soon."

Mark focuses his eyes, and a hot, forceful luminate wave emits from them. Everything momentarily turns white, but there is nothing. Everything is still black; he tries to blink his eyes again and look around to no avail. Mark starts breathing heavily.

Unfazed, the voice reacts, "Nice try, bright eyes."

Mark continues to try to understand where he is, "Am I suspended in space?"

The low, raspy voice just laughs.

Mark steadies himself and tries to look behind him, noticing he's lying on something. Mark turns around and hits the surface with his fist. A wave of barely illuminated energy emits from where his fist collides—just enough light for him to see a little.

Mark begins to feel very sleepy, repeatedly dozing off and opening his eyes. Mark focuses his eyes, and another wave emits from them, but this time, he swings his head around, yet still cannot see.

Mark, "Uggg!"

Settling Mark can tell the black floor is rough, like tiny pebbles on an otherwise flat surface. His eyes adjust a little; he can barely see the ground. Shortly, he can see several of his familiar spiders around him. One of the larger spiders jumps onto his head.

Back in his house, Mark opens his eyes to see an approaching paramedic. Ramses is by his side. Mairis, now calm, is still sitting on the floor in a semi-meditative state.

Ramses notices that Mark has opened his eyes, "You're back! How do you feel? The paramedics are gonna check you out real quick."

The medic has a little flashlight and is investigating Mark's eyes, "Do you know how long he was out?"

Ramses responds, "I don't know... ten, fifteen minutes?"

The medic turns off his flashlight and says, "Mark, I'm going to ask you a few questions. What do you remember?"

The medic continues evaluating Mark.

Ramses pulls to the side to give the paramedic some room. His hands are still shaking; he looks over at Tina, who is approaching.

Tina, "What just happened?"

Ramses looks slightly off into the distance while still talking to Tina, "That was nerve-wracking, especially with Mairis.

Tina eyes Ramses and responds in a concerned manner, "Poor Mairis has a panic attack at the sight of it."

Shaking and teary, Ramses fights to act casual.

In an unsteady voice, he continues, "It was like I could do nothing about it but watch him die!"

Tina reacts reassuringly, "Don't blame yourself."

The medic, finally putting his things away, continues, "Mark, visit the doctor for a clinical review as soon as possible. You seem fine, but if you like, we can take you to the hospital now, and you can see a doctor."

Mark zaps back, "I'll make an appointment, thanks."

The ambulance and medics are preparing to leave.

Tina turns back toward Mark, "Has that ever happened to you before?"

Mark rubs his face a bit, "No, I don't believe I've ever fainted."

Ramses, calming down, responds, "That was a scare; I'm glad you're ok."

Mark, referring to the last thing he saw while unconscious and dreaming where the spider leaped onto his head, mumbles under his breath, "Thanks to my spiders."

Mark takes a deep breath to steady himself, then looks over at Mairis.

"Hey, Mairis, are you ok?"

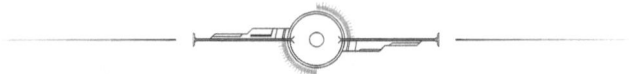

People are arriving at a rapid pace, even with an entrance charge. Party masks are everywhere. The masks that Mark made with the party imagery are selling out fast. Even the light rayon jackets with the party slogan are selling rapidly. Mark is exceedingly pleased that all guests looked reasonably attired. Champagne and martini glasses are frequently in hands everywhere as the rooms slowly begin to over-capacitate.

"That is an exceptional piece of depth, and I believe it adds a great effect to this splendid party of yours," a slightly thick five-foot-nine white male said with a prideful gleam, his brow showing small amounts of moisture.

His short blond hair is slightly messy yet matches well with a light beige sports jacket and dress pants.

Mark smirks, lifting his head loftily, purposely attempting to please and encourage while responding, "Hello, Josh; it is a little rough around the edges, yet most certainly exquisite. It looks even better with a little hard work. Careful on getting too close to it; wild animals within may decide to explore your world."

Josh chuckles. "Well, when I repay you in full, I want it back in excellent condition as it ever was, wild animals and all. I am simply glad to contribute toward the success of this fine event of yours; be sure to put in a good word for me."

Mark reassuringly moves his right hand. "Absolutely, the only thing that would change that is failure to pay... ," he laughs, continuing slightly sarcastically.

Josh responds, "I am determined to prove my creditworthiness."

Mark offers an alternative in the event Josh is willing to part with it: "You could always let me keep the piece if you need the money."

Interrupting them, "Did you set up that sequence? It is amazing, and so is this party. You must have quite the guest list."

Mark turns, attempting to locate the source. A lightly peppered, smooth-skinned young woman stands in front of him, pointing toward the wall video. Her hair is a shiny, shimmering black, complementing her dark green eyes. She is conveniently holding in her hand a nearly empty martini glass with a solitary olive.

Mark looks her over and says, "Yes, I did. If pictures are like a thousand words, it is a vast novel. Can I get you another drink?"

Isis's slightly raccoon-like eyes shift to the side with a slightly smirking smile, even though she is clearly thinking about Mark. The large screen is playing a combination of atmospheric, tech, and dubstep music mixed with famous art, famous places, music videos, and movie clips.

"Riveting, nice synchronicity. I'm Isis, by the way. Sure, I'll take another. Apple martini? Actually, this place is very quiet for the sheer quantity of people."

Mark presses his headset and requests an apple martini, then turns to Isis. "Isis? Like the Egyptian goddess? Nice name. You like the masks I made for the party?"

Isis turns and looks at him more directly. "I'm wearing one of the masks, aren't I? Are we to only show the side of us that fits the party theme?"

Mark chuckles, "Other than behavior befitting the party, you can show whatever side you so desire."

Isis turns to Mark, "And here I was, trying to be a better person."

Mark zaps back, "Always good to be a better you, but memories last a lifetime."

Isis sips the remainder of her drink, then, partially probing and partially looking for a reaction, says, "You could also render party entertainment more like a video game. That way, you can kill it with your computer skillz."

Mark, a little disturbed by that comment, makes light of it by joking, "I could have rendered guests and physical ones! I wonder, what would the choice of beverage be for the NPCs (non-playable characters)?"

Isis chuckles, "Apple Martini, of course!"

Mark laughs, "How did you know about my computer, uh… skillz?"

Suddenly, questions entered Mark's mind. Who is she? How does she know this about me? Does she know I create video games?

Isis smirks loftily. "You said you did the sequence of the video, and it's succulently hot. The music selection synchronizes smoothly with the video, providing a bit of mystery that prompts me to research the presented imagery. It's quite fascinating and suggests someone skilled in technology."

Isis pauses to sip her martini, then continues, "You have quite the crowd here."

Mark smiles out of the corner of his eye as if nobody really knows, "I like to think they have good taste!"

"I'll be back. I have to go attend to one of my friends," Isis jolts.

Mark slightly comically responds. "Uh-oh. Nobody should drink too much. It isn't wise and may require you to take over."

Isis smiles as she slips away.

Mark escapes to the bathroom for a moment. He touches up his hair in the mirror and is generally very detailed. Mark lifts a

Mark Izh-79 weapon from under his arm, checks, and briefly cleans the exterior. The teargas bullets are still intact.

Suddenly, interrupting Mark is a slight scraping noise from a dark corner of the large bathroom near the walk-in shower area. Mark briefly scans the bathroom when he notices the darkness encroaching on the light. He pauses to observe and verify what he is seeing. As the light loses territory, Mark looks at his arm. A plethora of goosebumps are up and down his arm. Mark visually hunts for the sound across the large bathroom. He slowly crept in the direction of the sound.

"It's cute that you think you can connect to dear old Dad," a voice said in a raspy whisper.

Mark swiftly looks toward the voice, but he can only see shadows. It's a dark corner. A little startled, he slowly moves toward the dark area. Nothing physical is there. Was there something in the darkness, or was it part of the darkness? The thought caused a slight uneasiness as well as a tingling sensation.

"Is someone there? Come out and show your face!" Mark says demandingly.

Mark thought to himself that he knew Olympus was a new city, but he had not expected such encounters.

The voice responds, "You're not real. What do you have to hide?"

Mark, now disturbed, walks over to where the voice came from. This is very startling because there is nobody, except him, in the entire bathroom. It was a 'voice'.

"What the? I have not heard a voice like that since old Gramps went crazy listening to them." That was not good, yet Mark was skeptical of the reality of them. "It sounded eerily similar to the voice when I was unconscious." He thought to himself as he exited the bathroom.

Mark's thoughts flashed back to his grandfather. An occasion in particular where Mark recalls having a strange tingling sensation that he couldn't shake. He attempted to follow the feeling and entered the garage, where he found his grandfather seemingly having a discussion. The discussion seemed one-sided, as there was no observable second party. Mark, as a little child, was perplexed and tried to listen really hard. He seems to recall that he was able to pick up some whispery voice, but his grandfather was also diagnosed with schizophrenia, so was it all in his imagination? On his deathbed, his grandfather whispered in Mark's ear, "Don't listen to them." This had a significant impact on Mark's psyche growing up, and he was never sure if they were real or not. He did not want to seem as insane as his grandfather's strange, erratic behavior was, so "not listening" to some 'voices' seemed like a way to escape this, but how could he ignore them?

Exiting the bathroom, Mark locates Ramses nearby. Perhaps Ramses heard the voice as well?

"Did you guys hear any unusual voice speaking?"

Ramses adjusts to the sudden interruption and then replies, "Everything seems pretty normal to me. What kind of... voice?"

Mairis is also present and zaps back, "I didn't notice anything other than us."

Mark explains in more detail, "In the bathroom, it was like someone was talking to me, but nobody was present."

Tina reacts to Mark with a slight chuckle, "You're not going cray-cray, Mark. It was probably just a friendly ghost."

Mairis laughs at Tina's comments, "Oh-my-god."

"Darn, so much for confirmation from others," Mark thinks to himself, then he responds with a laugh, "Yeah, I wish that ghost was more friendly sounding."

Mark slips away and makes his way into the kitchen-and-den area, which is also loaded with people. It is very slow-moving since he has to greet nearly every person as he moves through the party. Mark edges up to a finely detailed male whom he recognizes as Rae Osira.

"Rae, how are you this fine adventurous eve?"

Rae turns towards him and brightens his expression while reaching for a handshake. "Your auspicious event flows like a roaring flame yet runs like a well-oiled machine!"

Tina, who has also stopped to visit with Rae and Kara, "Nice choice of words, Rae."

Kara was clearly in a pleasant mood and carried herself as such: "This is great for Rae; too much work, not enough play."

Rae immediately switched to a semi-serious tone, even though he still seemed as though he was smiling underneath, "Yeah, my work-life balance is still improving."

Standing next to and almost, yet not quite, hanging on to Kara is Tina with a beaming smile. Tina chuckles in a generally seductive manner, clearly meant as a visual appetizer yet not directed at anyone.

Tina continues, "I wish office parties were this suave and artful. I must try to convince Siv to improve his atmosphere. Perhaps I should ask Mark to give him some advice."

Mark smirks a bit, then replies, "Thank you very much, and your attendance always adds something special, Tina." To Mark, Tina's typical behavior was always warm and refreshing.

Kara, "Mark, you too used to live in Memphra, correct?"

Mark turns a bit more serious, but still with an underlying smile, "Yeah, I'm still getting used to Olympus."

Kara, smiling, continues, "I'm guessing you attained your first software engineering job fresh out of college in Memphra. I'll bet that was a long road."

Mark's eyes light up as he corrects her, "No, I had a software engineering job before college. In fact, my father bought me a computer at 14, and ever since then, I have turned it into my career."

Tina reacts to that, "Way to take the bull by the horns. Very few teenagers start with a software engineering job."

Rae brings the conversation back to the present, "I've heard you have done some impressive work over at Dimensional Storm, is it?"

Mark, "I do take pride in my work."

Seductively gripping Mark's bicep while simultaneously stroking her upper thigh, Kara continues, "Rae could always use profitable friends in his investments; you should come over and visit sometime."

A gleam in Rae's eye clearly shows approval of such behavior from Kara.

Mark responds smoothly, "Most certainly, my friend. I'll check my schedule, and we can coordinate a sit-down."

Interrupting Rae, Tina interjects, "Mark, don't be a stranger." Looking at Rae and Kara, Tina bids them adieu.

With a light smile, Rae continues, "Yes, yes. Did you finish the landscaping in that video game environment... uh, Olympia, right?"

Mark zaps back, "Well, almost. It's coming along and will be finished soon enough."

Rae sips his martini and then reaches into his pocket for his tablet.

Rae, showing he pays attention, continues, "Sort of like the environment in this house and the landscape of its yard. The Qi is smooth. Flow masters like you always seem to design lush environmental scenes and landscapes. I'll bet it is effortless for you at this point."

Reaching Kara, Rae steps a little closer and snaps a few pictures with his tablet.

Mark notices Ramses a short distance away as he shakes Rae's hand. Like rocket science, Mark makes for an approach while Ramses looks his way.

"Mark! There seems to be a lot of available space if I were to crawl along the ceiling! I think the door guy is turning people away due to capacity."

Mark smirks at the compliment and pauses to look around the room. Everything seems on the surface like all is well, but his thoughts cannot help but go back to the events in the bathroom. Could the voice or ghost be harassing guests under the surface? Did I bring them to my party only to leave with an unwanted passenger? I hope my spiders will help keep everyone safe.

He continues talking to Ramses, "I have a nice profit margin on this event, I am sure. All the masks and jackets have sold out."

Mark looks towards the corner where the TV is playing financial news.

"Who the heck is watching that? My party attendees aren't exactly bottom of the barrel."

Ramses' face was gleaming, the oil on his face mixing with the sweat of his brow. Ramses laughed with a smirk. "Yeah, I noticed that. You should be sure to request business cards; opportunities must be among them."

Mark confidently responds, "I ensured the door guy annexes them."

Further meandering around, Mark noticed Mairis and Tina.

"How are you this fine festive moment in time?" Mark spoke as if time were not a linear subject with a very positive inflection.

Tina jumps, raising her hands in the air. "Mark! We are rocking out to your dubstep; we've already created a temporary dance area twice. How goes the flow?"

Mark nodded while slightly rubbing his chin, "I'll bet she's drunk." He thinks to himself.

"Shall we dance?"

Moments later, they were locked in rhythm, as best the girls could loosely maintain.

A few hours pass quickly as Mark tries to socialize with as many people as possible before finally returning to Ramses' vicinity.

Suddenly, Isis shows up, squeezing through the crowd. "Hello, Mark. I told you I would return."

Return she did; Isis, who is just shy of six feet, immediately smothers Mark. She is obviously slightly intoxicated, yet not quite drunk, which Mark is glad of.

"Should we escape to the upstairs room?" Isis seductively chimes.

Mark turns to Ramses with a slightly aloof raised eyebrow and a laugh. "See you on the morrow."

Isis casually rolls into her usual parking lot, where she locates her parking spot as if on autopilot. She quickly notices her brother Geb's large SUV in one of the free spots. There is nothing quite like a nice morning of brotherly razzing, she thought, mildly laughing to herself. The purr of her satisfying car comes to a halt as she swiftly makes for the townhouse.

Opening her unlocked door, Isis quickly locates Geb sprawled out on the crème couch with a large coffee, partially watching a sporting event.

"Ah, I see sister discovered her way home again."

Isis chuckles at the sarcasm while she locates a comfortable place for her purse. "Geb, what is of the utmost importance on TV that brought you to this abode of mine?"

Geb laughs and turns to look at her rather than the TV while lightly covering his mouth with his hand. "Truly amusing. How was he?"

"Mark? He was most certainly enjoyable. An air of sophistication mixed with a sort of cyber spinner." Isis gleefully elaborates while accessing the refrigerator for an energy beverage.

"Everything went according to plan then, good," Geb responds while casually examining his lightly unshaven face for blemishes in the small reflective statue endpiece.

"Well, you know. I usually get what I want." Isis smirks loftily while changing the channel.

Isis continues, "I did seem to notice a sense of mysterious possibilities in his house, in his eyes, and pretty much everywhere. It's fine, though; it's not like I know him well enough yet to pry. I got the distinct feeling that there is a lot more to him than meets the eye, and every detail is a clue. Really, that only added to the excitement of the moment."

Geb reaches for Isis' arm and clutches it with intensity and a tenacious grip. "I am serious. Some of those guys may be more dangerous, powerful, and ferocious than you expect. They don't always play like nice little gentlemen."

Isis swiftly turns and looks into his earnest and concerned dark brown eyes. She notices a slight tear mixing with the oils at the corner of his eye.

"Bro," she says softly, barely above a whisper.

Geb continues, "You know, I'll always be there for you like I am here now."

Isis smiles with sincerity and continues in a low tone. "I know, bro. I know. Mark was... cultivated."

Geb releases her arm with disgust. "Cultivated? You sure know how to pick'em. Rat race, here you come."

Isis jabs back, "Geb! Not everyone agrees with that."

Geb decides to cut the conversation short. With a frown, his facial expression shows undertones of lingering disgust and dissatisfaction.

Geb, "I must be on my way. Sett is waiting for me."

Chapter 5

Contact

Mark, sitting in front of his computer, is browsing through the gameplay schematics. The game is an MMO (massively multiplayer online game) in a massive gameplay map where each player will need to decipher symbols, communicate through symbols, compete with other players in combat, discover treasures, and even create treasures. Prized treasures will increase in value over time. While players can communicate with one another in the usual way, there are parts of the game where players will have a distinct advantage while utilizing silent symbolic communication. He particularly enjoys placing secret treasures and portals for the players to discover.

Taking a break, he opts to check his bank account for his most recent paycheck. Mark quickly picks up his tablet, sitting next to him. A high-resolution seven-inch mini tablet with a projector it was beyond excellent for the task. To his surprise, his account has minimal funds.

"What?" Mark mumbles to himself as he quickly browses through several of his private project accounts.

The large party profits he most recently deposited seem to have vanished. A tingle on his neck turns into a slight jitter as Mark decides to investigate the activity detail.

Scrolling through the transactions, Mark locates three withdrawals of various amounts. These withdrawals nearly depleted his account. Several thousand credits are simply gone.

"Fortunately, most of my money is in an investment account unless they got that too," he mutters again to himself.

The transactions are odd. The first transaction is from "You're not real." The second transaction is from "We will find everything out." The third transaction came from "There is nowhere to hide."

Mark is like, 'What the? You'll most certainly need a place to hide,' and he immediately calls the police as well as his banking institution.

"Check... t-h-i-s... out, Tink," Mark, slightly jittery, slowly states with a deep tone while looking at his tablet.

Tink, engrossed in something on the computer screen, slowly pulls himself away, "Huh?"

Mark, swiftly looking up, says, "You need to check this out." Mark is now calling the police on the sidebar of his tablet.

Tink swiftly rolls over to Mark in his chair. "What's up?"

Mark motions to his Smart Tab.

Tink examines the content and suddenly, with great intensity, scrutinizes the screen, "Wow! What the... ? Someone is playing with your head. A hacker, perhaps, but why?"

Mark on his earpiece, "I want to report digital thievery; who can I talk to? Yeah, I'll wait."

Tink looks up. "Let me know if they hack any of your computer equipment; I would love to investigate their handiwork." Tink then returns to his computer.

Mark, "Corporate security hasn't picked it up. Tink, you may be the man I need for this."

Tink suddenly fully focused, "Oh NO... I'm not going back to prison!"

Mark, "Can you check with security to make sure there hasn't been an infiltration?"

Mark back to the earpiece, "Yeah, that's my phone number. Yeah, that's my address. Okay, thanks." Mark hangs up the phone.

"I'm surprised that ANY corporation would give you access to non-public files," Mark smiles at Tink.

Tink zaps back in a matter-of-fact attitude, "Yeah, well, Ben's a pretty smart guy."

Mark chuckles, "You would've had a lighter sentence if you didn't sell it on the dark web."

Tink, now annoyed, "I'd like to think I've grown out of that."

Mark finalizes the conversation, "That's one way to keep a job."

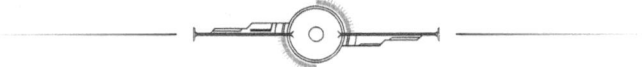

Reaching for his keys, Mark breezes toward his parked Acura. The sun is setting on the horizon, and a brilliant display of colors floods the sky. Mark is the last one to leave the office today and could not wait to get home. Suddenly, a loud hissing noise seems to come from right behind him. Instantly, it appears to stream to and fro around him and his car, sort of like the wind or a gas. Even more surprising is when it starts to talk.

A voice whispers in the wind, warping rapidly like the distance between it and Mark is swiftly changing, "Soon we will have it. You cannot hide."

There was no obvious physical source of the noises. A strange pressure sensation occurs on the back of his neck as the 'wind' brushes it.

"Now I know I heard that; what exactly am I dealing with? Is this a form of remote communication, or was the 'gas' actually talking to me?" Mark thought to himself.

Mark states out loud, in case it can hear him, "Don't you usually hang out in some corner somewhere?"

Driving along at a few miles over the speed limit, Mark ponders the odd encounter with his heart rate slightly elevated. It could have been worse.

Suddenly, Mark notices a strange pain in his head. It was like a headache he had never experienced before. Mark begins to waver, as if he is fighting sleep, even though it isn't the sleep he's struggling with. Mark's vision begins shifting back and forth between a daydream image of the road in front of him and a waking state. He looks down at his hands; there appear to be two sets of hands. His hands are on the wheel, but another set of hands are in a slightly different position, occasionally blending together.

A black mist descends over his eyes, and Mark begins to swerve, struggling to maintain control of the vehicle. He releases the accelerator. Barely missing an oncoming vehicle, Mark reflexively swerves to the side of the road, slamming on the brakes, where the car skids to a halt.

The pain intensifies and streams down his face. Reaching for his head with his hands, Mark connects deep inside his being. Sweat begins dripping from his forehead, which is soaked up by his clothing. Sweat then gushes in what seems like a small stream. Out of what appears to be a necessity, Mark pushes from within with a ferocity he has not shown for some time.

Very shortly, his physical face changes slightly, and his third eye exposes itself. The black mist rescinded nearly instantaneously. Utilizing his 'eye,' he can see all sorts of dark mists around him. In the near distance is a black, scraggly, straight-haired hyena. The hyena is not growling; it stands under a drooping bush-like tree with yellow flowers. A large number of golden moths reside in the tree, and a few of them fly away.

"What is upon us? What are these black gas clouds or mists? Why do they appear formless?" Mark ponders the sight he beheld, and the hyena is another oddity. A single moth lands on the hood of his car. Mark scrutinizes his surroundings; where are his spiders? He turns and surveys the insides of his Acura. Sure enough, there they are, several of the spiders he is used to seeing, yet they are not outside for some reason.

"Oh, there you are.".

Regaining his composure, Mark gradually presses the accelerator to continue driving home, "I'm not dead yet! You hear that?!... You won't get rid of me that easily!"

Isis casually sat on her couch, watching TV and dressed in her preferred pajamas, eating Cellato ice cream directly from the packaging. Isis takes a bite of her ice cream very slowly, removing it from the spoon so as to savor every micro detail of it and make the experience last. Looking at the ice cream container, this isn't the typical ice cream; this is luxury beyond the norm. Her beautiful hair is unwashed since she didn't feel like showering on her day off.

Suddenly, there is a knock at the door, but rather than wait, the door opens. It is Geb and Sett

Geb, smiling, points toward Sett, "Hey, Sis, this is Sett."

"Hey, Sett. What's up, bro?" Isis responds in between bites.

Geb, "Sett and I are going to a cabin up on Mount Zurich for a bit."

Isis responds jovially, "Wow, that sounds like fun."

Sett sort of loftily interjects, "A little change reminds us that we live."

Geb, stepping forward with a sly smile, "Why don't you come with us?"

Isis, suddenly negative, says, "Oh, no... I am relaxing just fine. Besides, I have to work on Monday."

Sett, stepping back slightly with his hands palm outwards, tries to reassure her, "A little vacay adds a little spice to life."

Geb approaches Isis from the foyer to the couch, "Come on, sis; it'll be fun."

Isis grips her ice cream; she jumps up and steps back to avoid Geb.

Isis, "Why did you have to ruin my day off?"

Geb keeps coming and opens his hands in a disarming motion, "Don't be like that; you said it sounded like fun."

Isis sighs and runs to the other side of the apartment. Geb chases her.

Geb slightly raised his voice, "Talk to me!"

Isis slaps Geb's hand, "Leave me alone; I was fine before you got here."

Geb grabs Isis and squeezes her arm, "Please, sis. Come with me; I need you to come with me. It'll be the kind of fun we haven't had for a while."

Isis heaves a large sigh, relaxing a bit. She responds in a much lower tone, "I have work… "

Geb also lowers his tone, "Just call in some of that PTO you never use."

Later that evening, Isis, Geb, and even Sett had long gone. A large all-white moving truck pulls into a parking spot near Isis's apartment door. Several men exit the truck wearing all-black clothing, including black gloves. They are wearing light vests over the black shirts that say "Easy Movers. We take care of everything!" They are wearing unrevealing generic ballcaps and high collars. One man pulls out an electronic door key (to the apartment) and walks toward the apartment door while the others prepare the truck.

Entering his house, Mark took extra care to be as silent as possible. These things seem to hear better than they see. Was it the ghosts of those so-called voices that plagued his grandfather?

"At least I don't think I am going crazy; this is very real." Why did his grandfather so desire to communicate with them? Mark often wondered what Grandpa would have been like without hearing them, which did not guarantee sanity.

"I must keep those annoying and intruding things out. These odd, highly aggressive voices seem to have something personal against him. They also appear to have malicious intent engaging in activities like theft," He thought to himself. Still remaining as silent as possible, Mark reaches for a nightcap before ending the evening in bed. He pours himself a drink, which makes some noise as he pours it over the ice in his cup.

Mark hopes it will not matter when, suddenly, from a dark corner, a voice says, "Found you!"

Mark, with a jerk, spills a small amount of whiskey. He turns toward where the voice came from. "Get out of my house!"

The low, raspy voice continues, "Very clever being silent. It won't work. Sooner or later, you will make noise."

Mark, very irritated, "I'll tell you what won't work. The little trick you pulled with my bank account. My bank will refund me the monies, and the police will hunt down your little hacker friend."

The voice continues calmly, "Oh, that? That's only a small sample. The police won't find him. We're going to take more of your valuables when you least suspect it."

It clearly did not feel as though "they" could "take" whenever "they" wanted to, and therefore, it was either studying him or not strong enough for a brute-force attack. Mark decided he has had enough of this 'dialog.'

Mark instead probes for information, "What have you done with Selene?"

The raspy voice replies, "She's enjoying what we have planned for her." Confirming they claim to have her.

"Now get out of here before I send my minions over there to finish you. I'd do it myself if I wasn't busy getting this beverage." With that, there is no sign of whatever or whoever it was.

Was this in his head? It sure did not seem that way, not at all. Mark carefully scans the room and whistles a tune. Still no response from what appeared to be the little 'dark one' or anything else for that matter. Rinsing his glass, he makes his way to his room while paying attention to every detail available to him.

With a small leap, Mark lands with relief in his silky-smooth memory foam bed. The memory foam is soft yet firm all at the same time, which makes for satisfying sensations, especially when Mark is mentally prepared for bed. Shifting states, his thoughts fade into the dream plane where Mark is waving to Tink while turning onto a small dusty path. Suddenly, he senses something—or someone, rather. It is Isis. She is somewhere around here, yet is not visibly present.

Mark continues down the dusty trail and then decides to take a momentary break to look around the immediate area. There is a solitary tree standing a short while away, alone, yet it did not look unhealthy, having vibrant green leaves. He thought to himself, Why is this road all the time? A dusty dirt road would symbolize a place of low population; perhaps it is not maintained. He looked at the road, and it appeared neat despite lacking a surface. Clearly, the edges appeared trimmed by someone not too long ago; perhaps it is a country road to private places.

In the distance, there is lightning and very quiet thunder, which seems almost to strike some rickety wood and stone objects. The area where this is occurring seems notably less hospitable. A few crows rest on various tall, unrecognizable objects. Was this the place where the "voices" are? Had he found them?

Mark approaches the location, and the previously silent crows announce his arrival. The "voices" do not say anything, yet that does not mean they weren't there. The crows could be their alarm system for all he knew. A drum begins to beat; it sounds like a large leather drum. He looks around and notices that the nearby spiders made no response whatsoever to the "noise." A dream catcher blew in from the wind, landing perfectly on a solitary wooden post that seemed to signify a sort of official entrance to the seemingly barrier-less zone, a single drop of water attached to the weaves of thread at its center.

Without warning, Alice stands next to him, smiling seductively. She always had a little lust in her eyes when she looked at him, and he had many dreams of her. For some reason, he seems to think she lives in a different thread of the multiverse. In his version, she did not physically exist. Even though it may be slightly odd, he found no reason to dispute this hypothesis unless she simply lived in the dreamscape. Tonight, she seems particularly pleased with herself. She reaches into her pocket and reveals a key, handing it to Mark. The key fits perfectly into a small spot on the dreamcatcher, but he doesn't turn the key just yet and instead carefully investigates the dreamcatcher.

Suddenly, a warm sensation came over Mark's eyes, causing him to open them to the usual ceiling. Mark, with a jolt, is wide awake, yet somehow, he desires to pursue that dream a bit further. What is that place? Is there friend or foe beyond the post entrance? He ponders as he prepares for work.

Mark's custom doorbell starts announcing the arrival of a guest. "How can I help you?" Mark jabs. Standing at the door is a clean-cut six-foot male with sturdy yet neat and warm thick clothing. Mark thought to himself, This guy's a skeptic, not really a bad thing.

"I am Officer John Thomas, and I am here to take your statement concerning the fraudulent charges on your account."

Mark thought it was a bit odd that a police officer physically visited him for invalid bank activity, yet he brushed it off. Perhaps it is part of an ongoing investigation.

"Wow, nice personal touch to physically take my statement," Mark continues, "Basically, charges suddenly appeared on my account. I am not really sure how they made those charges. Nothing was stolen or missing," Mark confidently explains.

John jots something down, "Did you lose or misplace any credit cards or personal banking information recently?"

Mark ponders for a moment, "No, that was the first thing I checked, and all my cards are intact. I could find no instance where they may have gathered personal information from me."

The officer looks seriously at Mark. "Have you had any suspicious contacts of any kind that may have had anything to do with this? Please be thorough and think of anything at all, no matter how small."

Mark looks slightly upward in contemplation. How is he to explain everything? That would be an odd story. "You know, I did experience someone who said, 'You aren't real.' What they mean by that, I am not sure, since everything feels very real to me. It was said in a suspicious manner, similar to what the credit card charges stated."

In a slightly skeptical yet serious scowl, the officer responded, "Really? Did you happen to notice anything unique about them? -Possibly a description?"

Mark is not quite sure about this; it was a voice, after all, and no visible description had been ascertained.

Mark responds, "No. Actually, I did not see their face; I only heard their voice—kind of deep and raspy. For the most part, I shrugged it off at the time."

The officer, clearly not sure if Mark was divulging everything, says, "Only a voice, huh? Okay, well, I'll add that to my report. Have you interacted with anyone who may have opposing interests? Do you have any opponents or foes that might consider doing this to you for any reason?"

In contemplation, Mark responds, "Well, I do throw some reasonably sized house parties. Anyone at the party could think of me as a monetary target. Other than that, I don't know."

The officer smiles. "We will consider all possibilities. Thank you for your time, and have a good day."

Chapter 6

Investigations

Walking briskly to his car, John peers to his right and smirks.

The detective accompanying him, Eurus, responds with a light smile. "Odd, wouldn't you say? That there was no description?"

Slightly frowning, John replies. "Not really."

Eurus, sensing that there is more to this, swiftly goes on, "It seems as though you should be the one to brief Kratos on this one."

After returning to the brilliantly reflective and large grid-like building known as headquarters, John exits his car toward the main entrance. The smart parking spots are so nice, he observes, with automatic energy shielding that protects the car from dirt and tampering.

Inside headquarters, Deputy Chief Siv Kratos is examining the daily work logs when his secure tablet notifies him of an incoming encrypted text. Siv's extremely short black hair is just slightly longer than his shadow goatee and blends well with his dark, bistre brown skin. His skin is unusually blemish-free and lacks the wrinkles of most men his age.

Siv softly reaches for his tablet and picks it off the enormous glass desk while relaxing comfortably in his large black and brown desk chair made of leather and dark brown wood.

"I've sent new atlas data of the incoming. Are there any new targets to investigate?" The other end of the conversation states.

Siv is pleased to have the intelligence. "I am mostly concerned with those that pose a threat to the quality of life here. The Dacian intelligence was good and very detailed. No further targets as of yet. Thanks."

Mark rapidly moves his mouse around the screen, occasionally utilizing the keyboard-like fingers of light. He is currently designing the internet interface for the game. He planned to have as much internet interface as seemed logical, including trading (or selling) game items. There is also an option for the hosting company to '3-D print' objects from the game and send them to players.

Suddenly, over the intercom, the receptionist queries, "Mark, you have some visitors. Garrick Nukis and Jeff Horus are here in the lobby. Should I send them in?"

Mark replies, "Sure, send them on up."

Mark, filled with anticipation, thought, "Was it Garrick from his dream?" He'd never met Garrick in the flesh. Mark's thoughts flash to the many dreams he had experienced while working together with Garrick.

Standing at the door is a tall, darker-yet-still-white male with short, wavy hair. Next to him stands another male with slightly elongated, slender arms, auburn hair, and dark green eyes.

"That's the usual smile. Garrick, my imaginary friend, has come to life and arrived here across space and time! What's up?" Mark remarks out of jest.

Garrick laughs. "Yep, I'm that Garrick. Nice to finally meet you while in the waking side of the universe."

Mark, "The dreams- they're happening in real-time, like a parallel dimension of our world?"

Garrick smiles, "Yeah... we have some vivid skills! Can you shoot lasers out of your eyes in the waking world?"

A smiling Mark chuckles, "Dacian."

Mark turns to Jeff and signs the question: "How are you?"

Mark had previously met Jeff, who is mute and communicates via sign language.

"What has been going down as of late?" Jeff signs his question with a smile.

Mark suddenly turns serious with a monotone look on his face. "I've had contact with some unusual events. A 'voice' or ghost - I'm not sure what else to call it - tried to talk to me at one of my parties, and some fraudulent charges mysteriously appeared on my credit card statement. Have you guys experienced any unusual activity lately?" Mark spoke and signed it at the same time.

Garrick looks at him with a serious yet pondering look while reaching toward Mark's tablet. "Can you show me the charges?"

Mark swiftly logs in to his bank account. "Here, look at the charge descriptions. One of them says, 'You're not real.' That is the same thing the voice said. I cannot be certain, yet it seems the same. It may have a connection."

Garrick, "Hackers for sure."

Mark continues, "Additionally, a voice in the wind nearly assaulted me and confirmed it had something to do with this by claiming it was 'only a sample' of what it might do."

Pausing, Garrick smiles, "Jeff, have you noticed anything?"

Jeff signs back; even if they tried to talk to him, he probably wouldn't have noticed. Smiling, Jeff signs to Mark, asking if he checked to verify that he was, in fact, 'real.'

Mark laughs, "Very funny. Perhaps I am not real? 'L-O-L' The question is, what does it mean by real? The whole experience makes me feel like I am going a little crazy."

Garrick responds, "Seems like everyone is a little cray-cray these days."

"If only we could get one of them to tell us what isn't real," Mark remarks in reflection.

Garrick, "For sure, but why steal something that isn't real?"

Mark, "There must be a reason they picked us."

Garrick, smiling, responds, "Perhaps we have something of value that they think they can get to. Isn't that the most common reason thieves pick their targets... Value means there is something real to be had."

Mark nods. "Right. Well, I'm not ruling anything out. We are different peas in different pods; perhaps this is how they try to push around the "other guys"?"

Jeff signs a response to that. "That's what I was thinking. If true, they are a gang, probably with a leader. We should try to find the leader."

Garrick motions toward Jeff, "We'd better get going."

Mark smiles, "I am sure I'll see you guys in my dreams. For some reason, what happens in my dreams no longer stays in my dreams."

Mark pulls into the circular, pristine white gravel driveway. With the typical crunching sound gravel roads make, he rolls to a gradual stop. Tina's small sporty convertible is already parked nearby. Looking at the mausoleum, Mark exits the car and approaches the stone structure. Mark recalls the mausoleum from his dream, and his memory flashes between the scene from his dream and his current view like a color lens. Mark continues to approach the mausoleum softly, taking his time for contemplation.

Tina is still in her car and notices Mark. She rapidly opens the car door with excitement and swiftly approaches Mark, meeting him in front of the mausoleum.

Tina, "Hey, Mark!"

The shrine remains as Mark left it previously; entering the mausoleum, he solemnly lights another candle. He talks to his father as if he is present, "See you soon, Father."

Turning towards Tina, he smiles, "Thanks for coming! How well did you know my father?"

Tina shifts her eyes with a smile, "Not well; I helped him find some local spots."

Mark beckons to Tina to follow as he walks around to the back of the mausoleum. Like his dream, there is a cellar-like door. Pulling out his electronic key, Mark touches the lock and opens the door. Again, there is a standard door below some stairs. Opening the inside door, Mark steps inside. Unlike his dream, inside is the expected storage area.

Small sunlit slits partially illuminate the dusty storage room. Mark scans the storage room; all of Thekaf's remaining personal effects that Mark didn't sell or have with him in his house are here. Most of the stored goods are memorabilia attained during Thekaf's life. Mark begins looking closely at the various storage containers and décor items.

Tina scans the room, realizing it could take a while, "What are we looking for?"

Mark, "I'm not sure, anything on a place called Earth or Ard?"

Mark skims through the containers, lightly tapping them as he goes one by one, when he comes to an old desk. An old but well-made, slightly worn file cabinet is underneath the dusty desk.

Akutra-Ramses Atenosis Cea

Mark opens the cabinet to a plethora of hanging folders and whips out his flashlight to ensure he can adequately see them. The folders appear empty or almost empty, which doesn't surprise Mark since his father digitized his records. Flipping through the folders, Mark sees one labeled Ard.

Suddenly excited, Mark pulls up an old dusty chair that makes a soft scraping noise as he drags it. Pulling the file, he places it on the desk, which has a thick layer of dust on it. Mark opens the folder onto the desk. There is a scrap of paper and a single old Polaroid photo. The post-it note reads "/backup0A1/ard". Mark looks up and scans the room for the possibility of computer equipment.

Mark rolls his eyes slightly, "Figures, it would be somewhere on some old hard drive."

Tina, "I don't see any computer equipment in here."

Looking back at the folder, He picks up the old photo, and Tina bends over to look at it with him. It is a picture of an old-style bicycle with wheel covers leaning against a relatively large tree. Underneath the picture, it reads "The Old Bicycle Tree, South of Vashon."

Tina suddenly lights up, "I know where Vashon is. In fact, I helped Thekaf locate that exact location."

Mark flips the photo over and looks at the back. Words are scrawled on the back more neatly than on the front. It reads, "Active Portal." Mark takes out his tablet and then searches for Vashon, resulting in a map of a small town near Olympus.

Tina, "It's one block south of Cemetery Road outside Vashon. I can give you directions."

Mark is relieved that he found something, "Cool, can you send them to my phone? An address if you have it."

Taking the folder, Mark turns and exits the Mausoleum with Tina following.

Mark turns to Tina, "Thanks for coming; it means a lot to me."

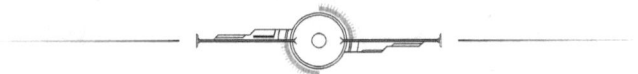

That evening, Ramses interrogates Draul in a large, secure, windowless basement, which is primarily concrete except for a solitary staircase. Slightly toward the back and in the center is Draul strapped to a chair. The dim lighting warmly illuminates the slightly muggy room.

A drop of blood lands on the cement basement floor. Draul's head hangs loose as he attempts to gain all the strength he can. His hands are bound behind him, and his feet are strapped to the chair. Ramses stands relaxed a few feet away with his sleeves rolled up, revealing his forearms.

"I know who you are with and what you are doing, so there is no point in playing tip-toe with you," Ramses firmly snarls.

Standing next to Ramses is a hooded person wearing a long black trench coat or duster with an elongated nose and chin, which is nearly all one can see of his face. The dimly lit room has an unusual degree of thickness in the atmosphere and reeks of sweat.

Ramses speaks slowly with a deep base, "Where are our friends? Why are you abducting them?"

Draul hoarsely whispers, "You're not real, and this doesn't matter."

Ramses, "You prefer to play outside the rules, huh?"

Draul rolls his head, "I won't say anything about it."

Ramses' nostrils flare slightly. "You're going to have a lot more than a bloody nose if you don't tell us what we want to know. You see, Anurah over here can make your life a bit more than 'uncomfortable.'"

Draul sneers slightly yet says nothing.

Ramses turns to Anurah, "Let's give our friend a taste, shall we? We'll show you something 'real.'"

Anurah lifts his hands and circles them toward Draul. In one hand, Anurah has some sort of small scepter. Within moments, scarab beetles by the thousands begin swarming from all directions toward the prisoner, who immediately starts screaming.

Ramses smirks a snarl, then says, "And they haven't even touched you yet!"

Within moments, the beetles are smothering his entire body along with the chair while Draul screams. Anurah again lifts his arms in a circular motion, and the beetles vanish.

Briefly looking at Ramses, Anurah again lifts his scepter. With the other hand, thrust a small ball of thread into the air. Suddenly, the atmosphere in the room becomes so thick it is nearly liquid. Ramses jerks and quickly adjusts while Draul slightly chokes and shifts, being clearly caught off guard by the change. The ball of thread slowed and suddenly burst into a luminous ball. The space around the light begins to stretch until it becomes clear that it is some sort of portal to somewhere or something.

Ramses smiles with dominant confidence, "We can abduct you as well. You have no idea what kind of amazing little places we can send you. Do you care to discover how real the virtual scape is on the other end of that portal?"

Sarcastically continuing, "You may find it a little piece of heaven."

"Wh-why don't you visit my friends with your parlor tricks and virtual worlds?" Draul coughs.

Infuriated by Draul's response, Ramses breathes deeply to control his anger. Reaching into his pocket, Ramses reveals a small eye dropper with some neon green liquid. "You may find this little technological marvel quite interesting."

Ramses walks closer to Draul, who is jerkily trying to find a way to avert the approaching encounter with Ramses. "This will sting a bit."

Gripping Draul's head, Ramses jerks it back, causing a slight snapping noise. Anurah reaches for the eye dropper as Ramses forcefully opens Draul's eyes. Dropping a few drops into each eye, Draul screams briefly until he realizes it is not at all painful.

"Look! Look all around you!" Ramses roars.

Draul apparently can now see a large quantity of various energies in the room. Ramses is extremely knowledgeable about the state of matter known as energy. "Do you know what happens to matter when it gets really hot?"

Ramses sneers and then scoffs, "You appear to have no idea what we are capable of."

Surrounding Draul, from what he can tell, are all sorts of energy forms. Many look very strange to him. Giant spiders spin webs for some unknown, possibly terrible objective while falcon-headed creatures peer into what seems like his soul.

"See the energies in this domain, this world. They don't take kindly to your behavior. Not only that, but we can chase you through hyperspace whenever we please."

Looking intently at Draul, Ramses continues, "You have seen who resides here, and now you are not blind to this place. Your friends would probably rather hide that from you."

Ramses grabs a chair with a sigh while observing Draul, sweat beading around his head. "I see you'd rather not give us what we want. Anurah, please."

Anurah aims his scepter at Draul, and it begins to emit some pulsating light, which also makes a slight crackling noise. Visible microwaves quickly reach Draul, who immediately begins to scream. Blood again begins to trickle out of his nose and onto the cement while he reels.

As John approaches his desk, he cannot help but notice the large, still-warm coffee cup with the familiar Starbucks logo on his light wooden desk, which has rounded steel supports. Next to the coffee is one of his preferred protein bars, a Nike 'Pharrell.' Smirking widely, he scanned the room.

Tina looks up at him from her computer and says, "Don't look at me!"

Then he notices Rhea with her long, flowing, nicely styled blond hair and her deep blue eyes beaming at him.

"You know. I am glad Kratos decided not to terminate you. You are exceptional, you know."

Rhea laughs, "Technically, I outrank you, so you better watch it."

Looking across his desk, John eyes his partner, Thoth, who is likewise studying John.

"Is there a high probability of the theft being linked to our new incoming guests? Them being the friendlies they seem to be," Thoth opens the conversation.

Nodding his head with a serious look, John responds. "So, it seems. Cyber-crime. They did actually attempt to steal money, unlike the incident at Dacian's place. There is no description, of course."

Thoth chuckles. "Naturally, they hide from sight, or it is simply not in their nature to show themselves. Possibly, they have a permanent locked closet complex."

Thoth is a finely detailed, slightly tanned white male with a very short-cut goatee. His medium-cut, light brown, and uncurled hair bounced effortlessly as he moved his head. His form is thick yet obviously low in body fat, covered by a finely tailored grey sports jacket.

John opens his laptop and begins writing a quick outline for his report after sipping his Cappuccino. Meanwhile, Thoth is investigating all the newly arrived residents.

"It is not all that surprising that 80 percent of newly arriving residents are blind." Thoth mumbles to himself.

John wraps up his report, which nicely explains the events in a way that his target audience would understand. "Mark is a new resident, and he was a target. Also, the incident at Dacian's place was a bit odd, and he was blind."

Thoth, still looking at his computer, responds. "They did not steal anything from Dacian. We do not even know what their motives were. Even though Mark is a new resident, he has been working here for some time."

John nods in agreement.

Thoth looks at John directly and then rests one arm forward on the desk. "Why do these guys think they can simply take? Don't they understand how the system works? They behave like a criminal raiding party."

Thoth thought about how much he liked living in Olympus. It's a nice place, with low crime rates, well-developed infrastructure, plenty of natural greenery, all set in a pleasant climate. Olympus even had nearby natural elements to enjoy, such as mountains and lakes. Having lived here for years, Thoth recalls a time when crime was nearly non-existent, yet nothing had ever been like the current wave of activity. It was like the wrong door had been opened, he thought to himself.

John interjects, "They seem to typically accuse their victims of this or that, such as not being 'real.' It appears as though they think they are somehow justified. Other such raiding groups have played within the rules, yet rarely pretend to be justified. Additionally, the justification is difficult to relate to. Mark seemed clueless as to their meaning, which means he does not grasp their intent, or he is not telling us everything."

Thoth's tablet notifies him of an incoming call. It is Tina. Thoth chuckles and finds it funny... Tina calling him from across the office.

"Dispatch reports a possible missing person's report. A Rae Osira has been reported as not being found and not showing up to any of his appointments. I'll send the address of his residence and other available details over. Rae is in my circle of friends, so you'd better locate him!"

Thoth frowns at John. "Missing person? Should we let the rookie verify that he is not simply out of the house on his own accord?"

John laughs. "No, I have been looking over the details, and I think we should have a look. Besides, Rae is an important individual to this community."

After dropping the report at Siv Kratos's office, they proceed to Rae's house. Rae lives in a gated luxury home community. Parking in Rae's oversized, sloping driveway, everything seems uneventful and undisturbed. John and Thoth exit the enforcer-issued Ford GT. Rae's gold concrete house shows no activity other than a lingering police officer as they approach. They swiftly pass through the police lines and examine the doorway first.

"No sign of forced entry. Perhaps he left his door unlocked while inside?" Thoth quickly zaps.

Whisking inside, they investigate further. Approaching them, Eurus is holding a tablet with notes. "Seems like a robbery; there is nothing of any value here. There is no jewelry in the house, and several blank spaces where furniture and wall objects were previously. Unless he decided to take his possessions and exit without telling anyone, it was theft."

John looks at him, "Prints? DNA capable residue?"

Eurus sighs. "We're still looking. There are lots of remnants pointing to Rae. No blood or anything."

John looks towards Thoth and thoughtfully asks, "Who would stand to benefit from this?"

Thoth is quick to offer suggestions, "I think of Mark, Rae was a good connection for Mark. Could Mark be the target?"

John nods and motions towards the door. "That is a good theory. So far, almost everything could be explained if they were targeting Mark. Except for what happened to Dacian."

John announces to the investigation crew inside the house, "We're going to interview neighbors within view. Let us know if you find anything interesting."

"Hang on. I am going to check Rae's records really quick and see if there is any reason for him to up and leave on his own accord." John zaps at Thoth as he makes his way to the car.

Following behind him, Thoth compliments him. "Good idea. There does not appear to be any struggle here, and thus far, no actual evidence of anything other than someone removing all the valuables."

Thoth steps aside and, slightly out of earshot, makes a call, "Looks like they nabbed Rae. We're investigating his luxury home now. I'll let you know more later."

"Wow, Rae. That IS surprising; I'll check it out," Ramses responds

"I'm still looking into Selene, but I'll do what I can," Thoth responds in a hushed voice.

"Just get me anything you can on my daughter, dammit," Ramses' intensity is sharp and swift.

John taps a bit on his paper-thin tablet. "Ok, get this. Rae is an independently wealthy technocrat and appears to have no present financial issues. He has several profitable investments, primarily in video game development, as well as a few other technology companies. Apparently, he has a high level of technical skill by the looks of the resume."

Thoth looks at John and breathes a profound sigh. "Let's check with the neighbors."

They swiftly commandeered several police officers, directing them like a military operation.

"We'll take the house with the friend." John points to a nearby house.

Thoth smirks and starts walking in that direction. "The Peregrine Falcon? Good thinking. They seem to show up at unique places." They quickly approach the doorway.

Thoth waves at the door alarm. A finely detailed elderly man opens the door. John looks him over with finite detail.

"You have a friend. Do you know him?" John points at the peregrine falcon.

The man lightly chuckles while observing the Falcon. "Fine animals, how can I help you?"

Thoth looks at the gentleman with detailed scrutiny. "We are investigating a possible robbery or disappearance of a Rae Osira. When was the last time you noticed any activity at the residency across the way?" Thoth says while pointing to Rae's place.

"Two days ago, I remember. I thought it was odd. There was an old rusty truck parked in the driveway. It was odd because vehicles of that sort don't frequent around here. Another very odd thing was a black cloud of dust or gas near his house. Very strange, like something in the air. The resident, I am only an acquaintance of, briskly left with another man, the driver."

John shows a pleasant partial surprise. "Can you advise on the approximate location of the... uh... truck?"

Pointing to an area of the driveway, the elderly man responds. "It was around there."

"Do you have a description of the man Rae was with?" Thoth continues while lightly rubbing his chin.

The elderly man smiles and gestures with his hands as he talks. "He was blond, short-haired, and slightly taller than Rae. He was wearing jeans and a white T-shirt. Sorry, I cannot be more specific than that."

John, "Did you happen to notice anyone removing furniture or other household items from the house?"

The elderly man looks off into the distance briefly before continuing, "No, no... You know, it was odd now that you mention it. A large white moving-style truck woke me up early that next morning."

John slightly smiles at the idea of a clue, "Any identifiable markings on the white truck?"

Elderly neighbor, "No, that was another odd thing; it was all white."

John smiles warmly, glad to have any information. "Thank you very much. You have been a great help."

Turning to return to the crime scene, John briefly notices that the peregrine is gone.

He looks at Thoth. "A black cloud?"

Thoth smirks, then continues, "Must be our new arrivals."

Returning to the driveway, they carefully examine it for evidence of any sort. The other officers return, having come up empty. Suddenly, John notices a small amount of black dust with a tiny bit of tire print.

Waving to one of the nearby specialists, John elaborates. "We'll get this analyzed and find out if there is anything like it in the area. No matter how hard they try, there is almost always something to find."

Thoth laughs with enthusiasm while holding his hands confidently at his hips. "I am surprised the elderly man saw the black cloud, though. You think we can determine the tire from the tracks?"

"Looks like it matches the description to me, but sure, someone will verify it."

John quickly zaps the descriptions to headquarters and then slips into the driver's seat. Moments after they leave the driveway, his tablet announces a response from H.Q.

Thoth grabs his tablet. "They've recovered what they think to be the truck. It is abandoned on the side of Iris Road."

John smirks while smoothly navigating the road and responds. "Let me guess, it was stolen, and there are zero prints."

Thoth chuckles while returning John's tablet. "Yep, nothing. They are still going over it, but nothing."

John responds with a sigh, "Let's hope that black material gives us a lead."

The car announces an incoming call from Siv Kratos, and John answers with his hand's free system.

John focuses on the wheel, "Hey, Chief."

Siv Kratos over the car speakers, "Any progress on the missing people?"

John rolls his eyes left and right while nodding with uneasiness, "We are learning a lot; this is a tough nut to crack."

Siv, "That's quite a few people missing; we need to get traction. We can't keep coming up empty on this."

John responds with a matter-of-fact attitude, "Understood."

Siv, "Do what you need to do, you get me? I don't care if you work in your sleep. These cases are starting to make me feel very uncomfortable."

John, "I'll put in extra time. If I could work in my sleep, I would do it."

The call disconnects. John briefly looks at Thoth, "I need a drink. Will you join me?"

Thoth is also serious as he nods his head yes, "Yeah, maybe we'll think of something."

John, "If I still smoked, I'd probably smoke a full pack right now."

Chapter 7

Friends

Isis is sitting on the edge of the comfortable queen-sized wooden bed, painting her toenails. The cabin room is quite large, with enough space for two queen-sized beds and an adjacent bathroom. The morning sun shines through the full-wall side windows to the right of Isis. In front of her and to the left, Geb is standing at the closed wooden door.

Isis has just finished one foot and proceeds to the next foot while Geb is becoming increasingly agitated.

Geb tries to project his voice as far as possible through the door, "Sett be reasonable and open the door!"

Geb leans against the door and notices no locking mechanisms on the interior side of the door. The door is made to lock from the outside, it appears.

An annoyed Isis rudely comments, "You're such an idiot! How well do you know these people?"

Geb sighs, "Give me a break; I had no reason to suspect this would happen."

Geb steps back and runs into the door, but the door is a thick, solid door that does not budge. Geb winces and drops to the floor then begins flexing his shoulder.

Geb, "Shit!"

Isis continues sarcastically, "Here you go, Sett; why don't you just have our tablets."

Geb turns toward Isis and lifts his hands at Isis, showing his desire for Isis to stop nagging him, "Just stop... We wouldn't have reception anyway."

Isis finishes her toenails and gets up.

Isis, "Well, at least we have a bathroom."

She walks into the bathroom and inspects the blacked-out window above the shower, but there is no opening it, and it would be problematic to crawl through broken glass.

Geb, "Sett, open the door so we can talk about this."

Isis, returning from the bathroom, observes the large glass wall across the room and notices a Peregrine Falcon just outside. The Falcon was obviously curious. Isis takes a deep breath and surges toward the window. A small thud comes from the glass as she makes contact with the window. Isis stumbles backward. The window isn't normal glass but rather thick polycarbonate glass.

The Falcon continued looking at them and did not scare away from Isis's charge. Isis takes another deep breath and runs into the window again. She stumbles backward at the thud. Isis tries again several more times. After several tries, unexpectedly, the glass cracks a little. The Falcon flies away, but Isis takes a break and sits on the floor.

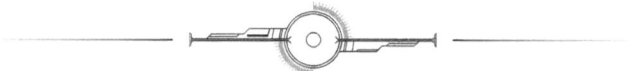

Mark is sitting in front of his computer at Dimensional Storm, considering the orientation of one of the symbol puzzles he had previously made. There is a knock on the door, and he turns to face it.

"Hi, Mark. How is it?" Ben says. Ben is his current contractor, and Mark is aware that his contract is coming to an end.

"Smooth as silk, other than the odd thieves," Mark sharply responds with confidence.

"As you know, your contract here is finished. The good news is, I have something. The bad news is it won't be here with us, and there aren't a lot of other choices. In fact, if you don't accept this contract, I won't have anything for you. You'd be on your own," Ben elaborates with a sigh.

That isn't like Ben; something seems wrong.

Mark ponders that. "Well, what is it?"

Ben labors to smile. "A new voice-activated space research program. It sounds fairly interesting, but that is all I have right now."

Mark laughs, darn if Rae hadn't vanished.

"Well, it does seem sort of interesting. If that is my only option, it sounds like I'll probably skill and destroy it."

"Applied Dynamics apparently does not need an interview. I guess that's good. In fact, I already have a contract," Ben spells out, partially upbeat, as he places a thick stack of stapled paper on the desk.

Mark appears slightly unsure while trying to analyze Ben's position on this, at the same time, finding Applied Dynamics fairly predictable.

Mark responds, "Right, naturally."

Ben continues, "If you agree, sign and return it to me. I'll advise you of where and when after that. Hope everything works out."

Mark, "A paper contract?"

Ben chuckles, "I guess they're a little old school."

Mark quickly dials Mairis. "You want to do something tonight, say 5:30?"

Mairis responds positively, "Sure."

Mark completes his work for the day and cleans up most of the project. Mark then reviews the contract and signs it. Placing his Vision ball pen's cap on the light-gray fine pen, Mark returns the pen to his desk while contemplating the future of this contract.

Paging Ben's phone, Mark advises Ben, "I signed it. Where is Tink, by the way?"

Ben responds with positivity, "Tink is already at the new contract site. The same one you are going to. It'll be a different department, yet he is there."

Mark drops the contract at Ben's office before locating the keys to his Acura.

Mark is looking forward to working at the new company, although he would prefer to take the C-level role with Rae. Rae's disappearance only makes it more critical that he investigate these people.

Mark turns toward the computer, still grappling with the ending of this work scenario. Fortunately for him, his contract gave him two months' pay at the end. If he picks up a contract right away, he would have extra money.

Later, Mark finally makes his way to his bed, like diving into a very comfortable pool. Shifting into the usual dream state, Mark finds himself with his arms holding Alice's nude skin close, but he cannot see the whole picture of her. Alice's face and hands are smothering him from somewhere; he has already penetrated her, yet it is all a jumble… a spaghetti of sorts.

The picture shifts and is a little unclear, but Alice is still there caressing him, and he is caressing her. It seems like he can do it remotely; he isn't sure exactly. The picture comes back into focus briefly before shifting again. This continues for what seems like a long time before they retire to comfortable, relaxed positions.

Suddenly, the landscape changes, and Mark finds himself near the location where he had been previously. It was obviously some sort of burial ground that possibly had a constant lightning storm and was home to various crows. The crows again make the same eerie announcements of his presence.

Mark decides it is time to find out what this place is. He pulls out the key and places it in the dream catcher. Moments later, lightning zaps repeatedly immediately in front of him. Mark suddenly and slightly stumbles backward, unsure of his safety. The crows fly towards a distant location in the stormy region. A short distance away, a mist of dark and luminous particles seems to emerge from the air. The particles combine to form a sitting elderly bald man naturally dressed in a thin, plain cloth. Drums begin to beat, and the crows return to the vicinity.

Mark comments, "Wow, smooth!"

The bald man begins to speak. "The one that seeks you is a dark one. He has issues with your silent sun."

Mark smiles confidently. "Who are you?"

The bald man smiles yet remains serious and, in a sort of methodical manner, responds, "I am Elder of the Beyond, spirit of nature's winds."

Mark, straight to the point, asks, "Are you human?"

The bald man responds, "I am a spirit of nature, not humanity. You may find a way to utilize the dark one's blind belief. It is possible to catch them off guard if you are true. As a matter of opinion, you can entrap them. We will also attempt to find them out." With that, the entire burial ground vanishes.

Mark opens his eyes immediately to a sunlit room. So, these are not the "voices" that were trying to steal from him then. Mark quickly moves to the edge of his bed and looks around his partially furnished room. He is immediately wide awake with a sense of inner satisfaction, as usual.

"This place still needs some furnishing," he mutters to himself. The "need" is evident by the clothing strewn around the floor and the solitary bed, stand, and desk. The rest of the house is also lightly furnished.

The nice thing about being an independent contractor is that he is free to do as he pleases throughout the day. After quick preparation, Mark casually strolls toward his Acura in his shimmering dress shirt and pants. Mark's shirt is dark blue with a pattern of shiny lines. It is quite warm today, and Mark did not notice any discomfort. Navigating his long trench coat, he positions himself in the driver's seat of the car.

Mark visited several furniture stores, yet was rather disappointed. He seems to have trouble locating the precise style and quality he has been looking for. Mark finally locates one store, which he suspects would be more of 'the same'—a local store called Jack's Furniture. After meandering in, Mark quickly notices some incredible choices that stand out from the large open-room display of the store.

"That collection just came in yesterday. Do you like it?" The salesman beckons to Mark.

Mark was a bit suspicious as to why a place like this would carry such obviously expensive furniture that looked a little unlike the rest of the store, yet he disregarded it. Others must have a sense of style, right?

Mark quickly selects some of the pieces, which are made of materials such as velvet, brass, glass, stone, and even concrete. The prices are very reasonable for their kind, causing Mark to examine them more carefully. After inspection, he found them to be entirely of exceptional quality and seemingly built to last, possibly longer than a human's life span. The furniture is scheduled for delivery later that day, and Mark makes his way toward a nearby restaurant for lunch.

The restaurant of choice is in the nearby megalithic towering shopping mall, which is surrounded by a small all-natural park. Mark opens the larger-than-life, all-glass door at the front of the main, mostly concrete, entrance and makes his way toward the specialty sandwich shop. Immediately, he notices a young female he had briefly met at his house party.

Her brown hair is long enough to reach her shoulders, complementing her deep-green eyes and full lips. She is reasonably tall with smooth-flowing curves, partially exposed by her relaxed white top and short pastel-green skirt. Standing and looking around, she notices him and smiles a sort of flirty smirk. Mark swiftly approaches while his arms and legs move in perfect symphony, with his head angled in a slightly aloof state.

Mark partially spins toward her and slightly cocks his head with a smirk. "Mairis, right?"

She smiles with seemingly internal satisfaction at the acknowledgment. "Yeah, that's me. You're Mark from the party?"

Mark smiles in response. "That's me. Did you like the party?"

Her body movement speaks volumes as she quickly says, "Oh yeah, it was hot."

Mark smirks at that. "Did you have a phone number? Perhaps we could rendezvous sometime?"

Mairis very slightly jumps and then smiles as she writes her number. "Sure, that seems like fun. Call me."

Mark closes it at that and continues to his lunch objective.

Reaching the sandwich shop, Mark briefly skims the menu. The waitress approaches Mark and seductively greets him, "Hi, Mark. How can I help you?"

He looks at her soft, flowing brown hair as it partially covers her smooth skin, which exposes a solitary beauty mark.

Mark non-aggressively yet playfully responds, "Hello, Kara, how are you? Where is Rae?"

Kara looks at him and responds with a slightly lower tone, "You didn't know? Rae is missing. He suddenly disappeared along with most of his valuables."

Mark turns serious. "Ah, that—uh, is unfortunate. Do you miss him now that he is missing? I'll bet you miss his... uh, valuables... I'll take the usual."

With that, she laughs and whisks away. Mark's tablet alerts him of an incoming text, and he quickly examines it. It is Garrick, of course.

"I am revisiting the location previously spoken of. I'll let you know what I find."

Mark thought about that himself. Perhaps he could look around the house in case there is more evidence of the intruders. Until this point, he had primarily assumed they were briefly visiting his home.

Kara approaches, and the delivery is fast, another good thing about this place. Mark admires the melting drip of fondue cheese smothering the shredded and charred chicken on the plate Kara delivers.

"Kara, the way you handle the plate suggests it may be magnetically attracted to you, or you are handling it via quantum entanglement," Mark compliments while flicking his right hand in her direction.

Sitting forward, Mark goes on, "Why do you continue to work here? I am sure Rae could find something for you to do."

Smiling assuredly, Kara retorts, "I only work here part-time. I like this place and the job. I get to see my friends, such as yourself. My connections are important to me, even the ones who respond via quantum mechanics."

"Ah... I spent most of my day furniture matching until I came upon Jack's," Mark casually reports.

Kara's eyes light up and slightly squint as she responds, "You discovered Jack's! Yeah, that place has a sort of psychic quality to it. It's like they already know what you want before you arrive. I am assuming you found something suitable then."

Mark smirks at that and responds, "That I did, that I did."

After a full day of furnishing his house in an orientation for good energy flow, Mark finds his way to his bed. Mark also looked all around the house and yard for evidence of the intruders, but he couldn't find anything to suggest that the strangers were not simply "visitors." He had even examined his yard, the trees, and the shrubbery. There was nothing unusual, and they looked nearly identical to his neighbor's yard foliage.

He lies on his bed, and his mind meanders, shifting into a state of sleep. Mark finds himself sitting on a couch, watching television. Channel 88 news is streaming, displaying an incident at a mall. Everything is very similar yet different, and there is no Channel 88 in Olympus during his waking state. It is still most certainly Olympus. Mark isn't sure at this point, yet if he had to guess, it was either simply a dreamscape or he had leaped into an alternate thread of the multiverse. He had been here a few times and scrutinized what little he could on previous occasions as well.

Standing up, he strolls into the dining room. The decor is a mix of stars and astrological symbolism, modern sophistication, and Egyptian hieroglyphs. In the corner is a large terrarium with various lizards.

Alice is standing in the kitchen, cooking breakfast. "Nice of you to show."

Mark, smirking, fires back, "Hi! I still retain the right to inter-fishbowl travel."

Alice looked him directly in the eyes; her deep green eyes seemed to flow like currents in the sun. Suddenly, she returns to her breakfast and attempts to fix it, turning off the heat. "Uuh."

Mark examines the scene a bit more. He notices a fresh fruit bowl lying in the center of the kitchen counter with vibrant, exceptionally fresh, and lacking blemish. The mango seems perfect, along with the kiwi, grapes, limes, oranges, and dates.

Alice reaches for the fruit; above the fruit bowl are some black cherries hanging from the cabinet. The cherries seem to have a sort of black mist around them. Mark suddenly realizes that she is reaching for the bowl because one of the cherries is falling toward the fruit bowl. He reaches out with swift, lightning-fast reflexes. Unfortunately, lightning speed was not enough, and neither did Alice catch it. The cherry landed on the dates.

The entire fruit bowl fades from vibrant to black, dead, and rotten. A slight anomaly or clear cloud seems to float away from the fruit as if its spirit is leaving. He is shocked by how rapid the decay occurred; it looks extremely unnatural.

Looking at Alice, she winces in pain. Grasping her stomach, she stumbles to the floor. Tears swell in her eyes as they roll. Mark immediately attempts to console her.

She mutters, "She's dead."

Mark is surprised that he seems unaffected. It is as if an event is affecting her via quantum entanglement.

Mark hugging and consoling her, "Who's dead?!"

Mark again with more forceful emotion, "Alice, who's dead?"

He softens and continues, "We'll find those bastards."

Chapter 8

Meet the New Contractor

Today is Mark's first day and orientation at Applied Dynamics. Here, he would finally see their faces. While Mark's car braced the curves with ease, Mark wondered about Tink. He would have been on-site for a few days and a good person to have a nice, nonsuspicious conversation with.

He is greeted at the door. "Are you Mark Kheops? It'll be only a moment. Dacian will be right out."

The gleaming large white desk greets him in the reception area, with slightly excessive sprawling patterns on the walls, flowing harmoniously with large gold plates announcing various successful results. Mark sits down in an elaborately patterned red chair with gold trim next to a large yet trimmed bamboo plant.

"Mark? Hi, I am Dacian Wilson, team supervisor and director of sales for the Stinger project. We'll have a briefing in my office."

Dacian shows Mark to his office; Dacian clearly knows the floor layout and sits down at his desk, his blind eyes looking slightly upward as he speaks.

"Welcome to Applied Dynamics. We work on projects for air, space, and sea exploration activities. For the most part, we help develop the tools and software to assist with proper exploration so as not to expose our fine citizens to the unknown," Dacian elaborates in his opening statement.

Dacian is tapping his pen on his elaborately patterned, large, blackened wood desk. Dacian's black hair was so short that it would not move, yet matched well with his dark, deep-seated eyes and prominent, bushy eyebrows. Dacian has a bright red pocket square in his otherwise all-black ensemble of sports jacket, slacks, and a tie. His bright-white shirt matches well with his untanned white yet not-quite-pale skin. Everything in the room looks fairly old-world with elaborate waves and frills, yet it was more of an intentional styling than reality.

Mark smiles and then says, inquisitively, "Thank you, sir. I don't mean to pry, but was your house broken into a while back? I saw it on the news."

Dacian's eyes look to the side as though he is in thought, pausing slightly before he responds, "Oh, yes, actually, that was my place."

Mark then purposely provides a look of anticipation, "I hope they catch them. Do you have more specifics on what I will be doing?"

Dacian shows a slightly unsure look, yet everything else reeks with an air of confidence and anticipation.

Dacian's eyes meander as he makes good use of his senses; he responds, "Well, I was planning on having you assist with the program positioning of the sonar and sensory for detection. Does that seem like something you can do?"

The edges of Dacian's mouth twitch slightly on his oily and slightly moist skin, revealing a hint of anticipation for Mark's response.

Confident in such a task, Mark considers this a way to get some inside information, "Absolutely, that seems very interesting. Thank you."

Dacian assuredly responds, "Great! Let's have Jaul show you around."

Dacian feels around a bit before pressing a button on his desk, "Jaul?"

Jaul walks into the doorway, "Mr. Kheops? Shall we?"

Mark smirks at the reference to his family name. "Call me Mark. Yes, let's do this." They immediately make their way through the hallway.

Jaul looks at him directly in the eye. Jaul's eyes do not meander; he clearly can see.

"Most of the facilities are actually on a security clearance need-to-know basis, but I'll give you the overview and show you your coworkers on the team."

Jaul is very slender and lanky. His long arms and torso are clothed with a blue striped dress shirt with sleeves folded at the ends. The shirt is equipped with a few pens in the pocket, a top button undone, and no tie.

Mark nonchalantly looks at Jaul. "A previous colleague came to work at your amazing facility as well."

Calmly, Mark made sure he didn't give any disloyal impression, "Perhaps you know him? His nick is Tink, and his legal name is Thisis."

Jaul smirks, "Yeah, I know where he is. He is on John's team. After the tour, I'll take you to him."

Jaul breezes around the offices, introducing Mark.

Mark pays extra attention to wall art, décor, and anything that might show signs of where they might be from or associated with.

Jaul gently pushes a partially opened door, exposing a neat desk and office area. Sitting in a mesh chair behind a desk facing them and staring intently at a large flat panel screen is a neatly kept male.

"This is Larkul. He is an engineer and works on the design of the actual sensors." Jaul interrupts the moment with a slightly lofty sense of humor.

Looking up, Larkul jabs, "Cold facts of what is there. This isn't a video game invention where we render the landscape to our liking."

Larkul has deep, dark, inset eyes, dark brown hair, and a slightly pale complexion.

Reaching beneath his thick glasses, Larkul rubs his eyes and then greets them. "Hello, how are you?"

Jaul then continues, "Larkul, this is Mark. He is another engineer, and he will be working in schematics."

"Any chance you can run that thing on my backyard sometime? There is some unusual activity back there," Mark chuckles jokingly.

Larkul manages a smile with a chuckle that moves his head, yet not much of his body, "Nice to meet you, Mark; I wish I could borrow it some time myself, Hah-ha."

Pausing, he continues, "While this isn't exactly a quiet place to work, it is a nice place to work." Jaul swiftly exits the room while thanking Larkul.

They walk past some additional office areas. Mark notices a door with a foyer with plants in the corners. The corners are darker than expected… black. The door is colored differently than others and is clearly much nicer.

Mark, "Whose office is that?"

Jaul suddenly became very serious, "You should never need to use that door; it belongs to the big boss, Chris Vocal. You'll probably never see him."

Mark nonchalantly tones down his curious expressions, "Ooh, okay."

Walking slowly past offices with windowed walls, Jaul points at the people inside. "That is Tamvis. He is also a junior sensor engineer. Any questions should go to Larkul."

Moving swiftly, he points to another windowed office. "There is Tarsus. He is also in schematics; he is busy right now, yet you might want to talk to him if there are any issues with the general layout."

Breezing on, Jaul opens one of the doors quietly. On the right and behind a desk is a male with a dark complexion. Deep eyes have a sort of darkened mask look, and the top of his head looks almost as if there is a dark skin spot merging with his black hair.

"This is Singh. He is an engineer and works on the motors... Must power the tools, eh Singh?"

Singh didn't even look up and simply responded with a slight smile on his flat, slender lips. "Must have. Don't want to be stuck without it."

Mark casually looks around the office. Papers, tools, and a wallboard of printed and scribbled drawings are everywhere. Mark notices something about the Titu Forest of Vular. The first names of locations he has seen. Generally, it seemed this guy either worked like a maniac or did not clean up.

Mark meanders, trying to get a close-up of the picture. He looks at Jaul, who is also looking right at him as his tour guide. Mark smiles to divert attention, then looks at Singh.

Mark casually gauges for information, "You have an interesting office; this painting is neat."

Mark looks around the office slowly to suggest his interest is of more basic curiosity as he takes a close-up look at the picture, but there is nothing further to be seen.

They quickly slip out and continue slowly, scenically, down the hallway. Jaul introduces him to a few more people working on the project. Finally, Jaul leads him down a hallway and into another large office area. Coming to another office with a barely open door. Jaul softly pushes the door open further.

"Tink, one of your previous coworkers is here," Jaul announces. Looking around the corner.

Tink looks up. "Hey, Mark, whazzup?"

Smirking slightly loftily, Mark responds, "What have you been up to, "do"? At least we're in the same building, huh? We can grab lunch one of these days."

"Cool. Now we can I.M. and e-mail from the company computer," Tink replies.

"I'll let you two chat. Stop by our project room so we can help you get started tomorrow," Jaul interjects.

"Okay, thanks, Jaul," Mark says, then turns back toward Tink, "What is it like working here?"

Tink, "I like it, it's casual and comfortable."

Mark gauging for names, "Who do you work for?"

Tink releases a smiling sigh, "John... John Coords."

Mark pauses and looks at the door, listening intently. He pays close attention to his senses to make sure Jaul is gone. Mark then lowers his voice.

"Did you notice anything odd about this place?"

Tink lowers his tone to match. "Thus far, the only thing odd about it is that most of the projects are on a need-to-know basis."

Mark smiles nonchalantly and quietly says, "Keep your eyes peeled and let me know." Slightly raising his voice, Mark continues, "Well, you have a great day. I'm sure we'll talk later."

Exiting Tink's office, Mark looks carefully around, but Jaul is nowhere to be found. He softly walks back to Chris Vocal's door. Slowly looking carefully at the door, Mark listens to see if he can hear anyone inside. Reaching the handle, Mark turns it softly and slowly, but it is locked.

Mark notices again that the corners of the foyer are black. He looks around to be sure nobody is within visibility and then softly creeps close to one of the corners of the entry area. The corner appears covered with black dust, especially behind the plant.

Suddenly, a low, raspy voice from the darkness says, "You shouldn't be snooping around."

Jolting Mark scans the area again, but no one can be seen. He exits and meanders back to where Jaul said he would be... in the project room. Jaul notices his entry and immediately points him to his desk.

"Here is your office, and while you do not have a window view yourself, the view is right across the hallway, immediately visible through the glass doors."

Mark smiles, not sure that they even considered that, "Great! Thanks for thinking of me."

Mark thought the solid dark-gray wall looked nicer than the other pastel yellow walls. The wall is adjacent to a single glass wall with a door. Mark arranges his desk and checks the contents of his hard drive.

Mark swiftly grabs his jacket and makes for his Acura. As Mark reaches for the ignition of his car, he suddenly becomes aware that someone is nearby. Slowly, he lifts his head and stealthily scans the area when suddenly there is a light knock on the window. It is Mairis.

Mark sighs with relief as he opens the door. "You came here to my work parking lot? I was on my way to pick you up."

Mairis chuckles and moves into a comfortable position resting on the exterior of Mark's car. "It's easier this way. I have my car with me. Can we drop it at your place?"

"Sure, my place is fine, but I was looking forward to seeing your place." Mark zaps back while still processing everything.

Is she hiding something, or is she simply planning to stay at my place? Mark wonders.

"There will be a time for that. I hope that is acceptable." Mairis brushes herself off nonchalantly.

Mark nods and gestures to the effect of 'no problem.'

After dropping off Mairis' car, they make their way to the nearby theater.

Upon parking the car, Mark looks at Mairis. "You like movies, don't you?"

Turning and looking him directly in his shimmering eyes. "Yes, yes. Let's watch a movie."

The movie list has a variety of options brightly scrolling on the screen, complete with movie art and slogans. He mumbles, "Mandelbrot Jumper, States of Matter, The Pattern Repeaters, White Nose Plague, Masters of Khi, Acuteness of Vision, Kumonosu." Mark then continues, "Any preferences? I am sort of leaning towards Masters of Khi."

Leisurely strolling, Mark studies the design of the theater. It is clearly one of Ramses' designs, with many pathways leading to several megalithic central points in a web-like pattern. Nearly everything is concrete, colossal, and sort of like a connected net as opposed to one enormous building. It is not actually a single building, yet it displays the idea that the participating buildings are connected while other nearby buildings are clearly not connected. The style is perfect for the theater, which always had several shows playing.

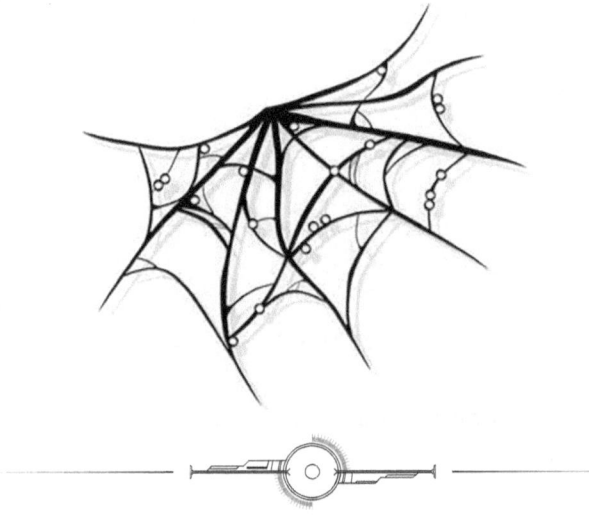

Admiring an abstract wall art piece that Mark recently installed, Mairis shows genuine interest, clearly smothering the canvas's details.

Mark moves close and, in a low tone, says, "You like it? It seems to sort of extend from the wall and into a possible other realm somewhere in its depths, doesn't it?"

Mairis turns toward Mark. "I see that."

Mark reaches around her head, touching her cheek. He guides her face toward his mouth and immediately begins to explore her mouth, among other parts. Mairis immediately appears to sort of melt in his embrace. Turning her back toward the wall, she slightly stumbles backward. Mark immediately responds by shifting toward the wall where she rests against it. She tugs on Mark's torso area.

After a short while of exploring the wall and several dimensions of each other's body, Mark pushes her in the direction of his giant bed. Mairis responds quickly with exuberance, pushing Mark onto the large bed while a few drops of sweat make their way toward the lower portion of her chin.

Waltzing into the new office, Mark has the taste of his morning espresso lingering on his tongue. He sits down at his desk, turns on his computer, and begins perusing the document that had been purposely placed on his keyboard. Looking up, Mark notices Jaul slip in and meander a short way from the door.

"Morning, Mark. I am going to help you get started on our new project. Understand, we are working on the next-generation product, and the current version is selling well from what I hear," Jaul cheerfully elaborates while nursing a cup of coffee.

Mark notices Jaul do a casual scan of his personals and acknowledges to himself that he would need to be careful.

Jaul is dressed pretty much the same as yesterday; only the shirt has a slightly different yet similar pattern. Jaul's hair hangs past his ears yet is short enough as to not reach his shoulders, and it is a bit more frazzled today with no real shine.

Mark gleamed back. "Morning, and here I was, going to try to dive in and understand it myself. Awesome."

The two of them turn suddenly to acknowledge the arrival of Dacian.

"I am singing in the rain today!"

A beaming Jaul responds with nearly his entire body. "What is up?"

Dacian looks at Mark and then at Jaul with enthusiasm and says, "Moments ago, I was in a board meeting. Sales of our explorer class are up 20 percent from last month, and it sounds like we are going to have some new clients! I presented it to Darkwaters, the underwater resource miners, and it was like selling itself. It felt like I was practically stealing the deal. There is potential for so much profit."

Mark smiles with a bit of a chuckle. "Great! So, you will want the next-generation vehicle that we are working on, which will allow you to make some more stealing deals."

Dacian smiles in confirmation. "Absolutely, glad to have you on the team."

Jaul was still looking at Dacian. "I was showing Mark the part he will be working on so he can get started."

Dacian smiles and responds animatedly, "Of course, of course. I had to tell you guys how things were going. Sounds like we are going places today! Talk at you guys later!"

With that, Dacian strolls out of the office. Jaul turns to Mark.

"Great news, eh? How about you look over the Stinger project's system files and get to know it for now? Let me know if you have any questions at all," Jaul turns quickly and makes for his own office, likely to investigate the newfound news.

Mark opens one of the project's PDF files and begins coming to grips with the product when his instant messenger starts flashing. It is Tink asking him how it was going, and Mark responds in kind.

Tink then messages, "Did you hear from Dacian about product sales? Great, eh? Good for business, good for our contracts."

Mark responds, "Yeah, that is good, for now anyway. Did you look around? Did you notice anything unusual?"

Tink responds with a frown, "'Do'! No. Nothing unusual. Only the usual company business to make the product and sell it. I, for one, am glad they are going to make some money so I can keep my contract and possibly get an extension when it is up."

Ah, Tink is going with the pocketbook. Mark did not blame him for that.

Mark then responds, "Okay, well, several people have had things stolen. I can tell you about it later."

Tink responds, "You and your conspiracy theory. Who really cares if blind people are working here? Wake up and smell the coffee, bud." With that, Tink places his instant messenger in do-not-disturb mode.

After a few minutes, Mark gets up and carefully looks around, but nobody is meandering in the hallways. Mark casually walks toward Chris Vocal's door. He acts confidently to avoid suspicion. Chris's foyer is the same as it was before. Rather than re-visit Chris' door, he continues to Singh's office. The door is open, so he stands in the doorway.

Mark decides he can look less suspicious if he talks about his job first, "Hey, Singh? What will the power requirement be for the motor on the next model?"

Singh jolts; he was clearly not expecting Mark, "Oh, hello, Mark. Power? Let me see…"

Singh looks back at his computer and pulls up a few files.

"The plan is to increase the available wattage to 200 on the standard unit, so the motor has a little more go. You're referring to wattage on the underwater propulsion, correct?"

Mark recalls the documents he reviewed so as to ensure he can appropriately respond, "Yeah, I'm looking at the new power supply and what kind of upgrade makes sense for the sensors."

Singh smiles while responding, "Cool, cool. I am glad to help with anything."

Inquisitively, Mark turns to his real objective here and points at the picture of the Titu Forest:

Mark, "Out of curiosity, where is the place in the picture?"

Singh's face lights up, and suddenly, he is in an apparent good mood, "Oh, that? It's from a cool old video game I used to play... Darkened Dawn."

Mark cools his jets with an inconspicuous compliment, "It's pretty cool artwork... Well, thanks!"

Singh, "Anytime!"

Mark slips back to his office, noticing how empty the hallways are. Suggesting people do not need to leave their offices much, or they work at different hours, which is good for him.

Mark reviews the schematics, plans, and objectives for several hours before zipping up his jacket. Wondering what Tink is up to, Mark zaps him an instant message.

"Tink, my friend. Why are you here so late?"

Tink responds with a sunglass smiley and, "OT pays the bills with a little extra."

Mark smiles at his hard-working friend's candor, "What about we make the leap to the Cyberpad?"

Tink's response took a few moments, "I would like to; however, I must linger with blood."

Mark chuckles at Tink's wording, "Did you use a time machine recently? Blood really? In the modern era, we utilize DNA to determine TRUE relatives. The gene is far more accurate and correct than the old archaic term 'blood.'"

Tink quickly zaps back an 'lol' and a laughing smiley. With a quick, short, snort-like laugh, Mark continues, "Really? The term 'blood' was used when people did not know much about the subject. Parents often don't even have the same blood type! Well, anyway... have fun with the relatives!"

Mark decides that it might be nice to meet with some of his new affiliates and swiftly begins instant messaging Larkul to gauge his current state.

"How are you this fine evening?"

Larkul replies after a slight delay. "Doing well. It has been busy, yet seems to be coming together."

Pondering his next query, Mark quickly responds. "What are your plans after work? Perhaps we could review project notes and socialize a bit."

Larkul responds with a frown smiley. "I must crash, man; I have been working long, hard hours."

Mark smirks at that, "That is why you optimize your sleeping patterns. So, you sleep less and live more without the crash later."

Larkul responds quickly. "Yeah, well, that's easier said than done. I push it a bit at times. Have a nice evening. Perhaps later, I'll take you up on that."

Chapter 9

Not Your Typical Fight

A relaxed, Mark sits at his computer station with Garrick standing behind him, looking over his shoulder. Mark clicks a retro emulator icon, and the primitive but well-done graphics load for Darkened Dawn.

Mark explains why he is loading the game, "The fictitious reference was the only thing I could find on Vular or Titu Forest. A reference is just an area of the game. I was hoping to uncover where it came from, but so far, no luck."

"A myth in a video game, weird," Garrick comments.

The computer screen plays the introduction... Legend has it of a great magical kingdom that survived cataclysmic events.

Garrick continues, "Any connection?"

Mark, correlating the elements of the game, replies, "There is. Inside the game, the player encounters black mists. It's a pretty unique game.

Mark minimizes the game and opens his browser to a game forum. Mark points to the answer on the screen.

ONLINE GAMER #1, "Question: How do I get past the black mists? They're immediately hostile, so I have to fight. I kill some of them, but they always kill me in the Titu Forest."

ONLINE GAMER #2, "Answer: Once you obtain the sword of Darthor, you gift it to them, and they will become your allies. You cannot kill all of them, as far as I know. They will always eventually surround you."

Garrick undaunted, "Never know how much of the myth is true. It seems odd for them to have mythic places from a video game in that office."

Mark, "For sure."

Mark quickly, "Should we hit it to the Cyberpad?"

Garrick made sure he had everything before making for the exit, "Yeah lets, I'll see you there."

Cyberpad is a hot spot for internet, LAN games, energy drinks, and coffee—among other things.

With that, Mark grabbed his keys and trench coat while making for the door, all in one smooth stroke.

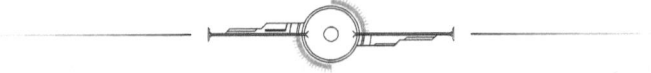

The solitary waiter/bus girl drops off several twenty-four-ounce energy drinks while making seductive eye contact with Garrick.

"You're awwe-some sizzles, thanks. When do you get off so you can linger with us?" Garrick responds to her eye contact with a confident yet enthusiastic tone.

Looking down at the table, she responds in a matter-of-fact way, "I work late tonight. Here's my number, though." The waitress has her number ready on an old-school piece of paper.

Mark chuckles; she already had it ready. What was her plan?

Mark, "She's already dressed for success, smooth move."

A grinning Garrick says, "Yeah, I noticed."

The decor of the Cyberpad is as futuristic as anything, yet Mark can see slight undertones of a time before the computer. Everything has smooth lines and curves, rarely any excessive frill, yet with a few appealing patterns. The cybernetic wall art is very interesting and is painted directly onto the walls in bright, vivid colors mixed with dark tones. The arms on the low chairs and couches have a sharp edge that swoops in a curved manner directly into the chair, which appears to be a single-piece assembly. The table appears to be vortex-inspired, while the automatic glass sliding doors have curved corners. Looking up, the ceiling is further than ten feet. A giant bronzed falcon, purposely created with smooth surfaces rather than realistic detail, is suspended in midair.

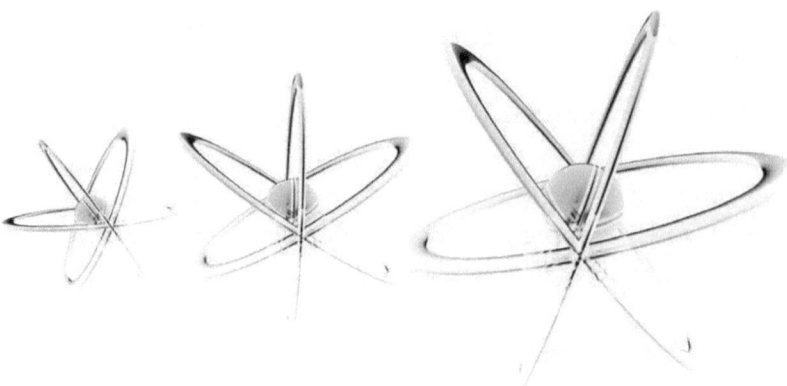

All three of them have their tablets out, and Garrick has his laptop as well. Mark displays his tablet browser on the table, which has a display-enabled surface.

"How's my friend from across space-time?"

Garrick, "Just dreamy."

Mark smiles at the reference, then gets comfortable, "Did you search for activity?"

Garrick responds in a slightly negative tone while playing with his short yet wavy hair, "You said they claimed that the police would not find anything, so chances are it will be hard to detect. I did investigate a bit, though, and did not find anything unusual. I did discover that missing persons incidents have been up significantly in the past few months."

Mark, with a look of feigned shock, "What is this? An invasion? Missing persons on the rise? We may need reinforcements."

Garrick, "Let's hope not."

Mark sits forward and picks up his tablet.

"I pulled up some nearby addresses, Alice, and I obtained from a supplier. Since I have extracted them from my dream, they may not be exact. Let's see if we can correlate them to anyone. Garrick, see what you can find about Applied Dynamics," Mark says in a down-to-business attitude.

Garrick mutters, "Applied Dynamics? Why them?"

Mark looks at him. "That is my next contract, suspiciously my only option. Jeff, help me check out Dacian and some of these addresses."

With that, they pursue the targets when Mark's tablet alerts him of a call. In a smooth, overly friendly tone, Mark answers, "How are you? What did you do to your hair? It's black."

Mairis laughs seductively, suggesting an "if you only knew" tone, lightly touching her face and mouth. "Yes, I did a makeover. Where are you?"

Mark is thinking, "nice," then smirks and says, "We are at the Cyberpad. Why don't you drop and linger?"

Mairis smiles, her full lips forming an assured pout. "I'll do that; see you in a bit."

Mark returns to his browsing. He has located Dacian and swiftly skims for anything he could find, even doing a two-credit address search.

He looks at Garrick. "Find anything?"

Garrick looks at him studiously and begins, "Applied Dynamics is a small to medium company funded and owned by an independent yet-to-be-determined investor. The CEO goes by Chris Vocal, who is presently worth five million and owns several homes. Get this: the CFO is a blind person by the name of John Coords, and everything must be translated into braille for him. Dacian Wilson, the guy you are looking up, is a managing director at the local manufacturing facility. Did you get his address?"

Mark nods. "Yes, and that address is on my address list!"

"Chris Vocal's address is a neighbor to one of your addresses on the west side," Garrick joins in.

Mark lightly rubs his face in contemplation, "I suspect that 'blindness' is not actually a disability to these... uh, entities. Which is actually an attitude we could learn from if they were a bit more friendly."

Garrick smiles, "I like your thought process; we should always learn from everything. Even the opposition."

Garrick turns back to his tablet and continues, "Applied Dynamics designs and develops, as far as I can tell, space-air-sea equipment for all sorts of purposes. Your new contract may be with people who are associated with the crazy voices." They continue for a bit on that topic.

Turning toward the door, Mark notices Mairis approaching. Her long, now-black locks of shiny hair move in a slightly yet smooth-flowing fashion while her short black dress hugs her curves, allowing some imagination as she streams toward them. As she gets closer, Mark cannot help but recognize the similarity to Alice.

Mark smiles, "Mairis, you're here!"

Mairis beams, "Hi, 'do' what is happening on the flip side?"

Mark quickly signs a translation for Jeff even though Jeff usually can read lips.

Garrick smiles. "Just doing a bit of research, hopefully on our harassers."

Mairis immediately sits down as if she is nearly in the same physical spot as Mark, gripping him while she removes her white and light green leather jacket to reveal her nice little black dress further.

Mairis's eyes are slightly raccoon-like from her eyeliner, yet she wore only light amounts of makeup, including shimmering lavender lipstick, complementing her plump, full lips. Her feet are covered by flat black leather shoes that wrap around her feet, making them look like a second skin with a neon-green atomic symbol on the side.

Mark quickly jabs, "You like the Cyberpad, Mairis?"

Mairis smiles warmly as she pulls out her minitablet. "Absolutely, it sizzles."

Mark, "What's Tina up to?"

Mairis looks back at Mark, "She's visiting her brother. She should be back tonight or tomorrow."

Jeff quickly starts signing to Mark.

Mark chuckles, "He likes your tab. Is it the one with the projector?"

Mairis laughs loftily. "Yes, I just upgraded it. It's so awesome."

Mark turns to Garrick and continues, "It is a bit odd that these people have minimal history available. See if you can find anything further. Garrick, don't you think the Applied Dynamics website is a bit uncreative?"

Garrick swiftly moves his hand around his tablet screen. "Yeah, most certainly. Nothing special about it; there's not much company art beyond the logo. It's a website that most anyone could very quickly throw together."

Mark did a traceroute on the web address and then handed Garrick half of the nodes on the list directly to his tablet. "Check those out, I'll check these."

After a few moments, Garrick states in a matter-of-fact tone, "This node list goes out of state... to California."

Mark looks at him. "Yeah, it's a Web hosting service, a cheap one too... matching the website. They didn't even design their own website, much less host and manage a web server. All that Internet technology too complicated for them?"

They all laugh at that, and Mark continues, "Hyperspace is probably messing with their bat senses."

They continue laughing for a bit.

"It is possible that they are all a front for something else or very recently constructed. The history seems very limited."

Garrick then looks at Jeff. "We should get going. I need to work on the morrow."

Jeff signs back, "Good idea; I should get home as well. I have some video games that need completing."

Mark turns to Jeff. "What do you do for work?"

Jeff signs back, smirking like he owns it, "I test video games."

Mark sat back, opening his mouth slightly, his whole body chuckling. "Ohhhh, that is smooth. What a tough job that must be. Is it awesome?"

Jeff's whole body was nodding yes as he spelled out Y-E-S.

Mairis laughs. "I'm so envious."

Mark turns to Mairis. "You want to 'hit it' to my place?"

She looks at him, locks lips, and then mumbles, "The plan I was hoping for."

Mark turns toward Garrick and Jeff. "Okay, do's, we'll 'check-it' later."

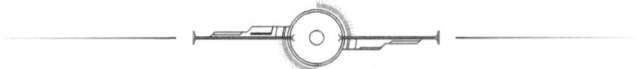

It is a peaceful night sky with nary a cloud. Ramses's beautiful two-story home at the end of the enormous walkway has only a few lights on while Ramses is away on business. A warm yellow light illuminates the doorway on his nicely sized porch. Another large motion-sensitive flood-style light can be clearly seen attached to a tall metal post, which is currently off since nobody is near enough to trigger it.

The whisper of the crickets and typical small wildlife of this well-maintained, enormous rolling yard surrounding the house can be heard. The sun had fully set, leaving the stars to shine their brightest. The moon glow keeps the area barely illuminated, but there are several dark shadows in the corners, under the trees, and from the shrubbery.

Suddenly, an unnaturally dark shadow creeps from the road, covering the driveway, yard, and everything in its way with absolute black shadow-like darkness. It creeps toward the house at a rate that slowly increases until it reaches the porch. The floodlight does not come on, and nothing is there to alert the somewhat distant neighbors that anything is amiss.

The utter black reaches the porch light, still beaming bright. Then, as the darkness covers the light, it fades to a black light before ultimately going out. The floodlight is also covered but has not been triggered and is still off. Everything appears as though matte black paint has covered every crevice.

The dimly lit hallway inside the doorway has a very advanced LCD alarm and a smart home control panel on the wall. The LCD panel reads ARMED on top of the screensaver. The black shadow creeps in, covering the doorway's interior, and then continues covering the walls. The darkness reaches the smart home control panel. Covering the panel, the screen dims but can still be seen.

Suddenly, the smart control panel scrambles, then reads 'unlocking front door.' The front door's advanced locking mechanisms unlock noisily. The smart panel then reads disarmed before going completely black from the darkness.

The door handle slowly opens. Then the door slowly opens, revealing an all-black figure wearing little flashlights on the sides of his head, black nitrile gloves, and a black mask. The figure is so completely covered in black clothing that his eyes cannot even be seen. Behind him is the slight outline of a large all-white moving truck, which can only be seen because the powerful floodlight was triggered and is now emitting a faint glow. The truck appears to be the same truck the movers used at Isis's apartment. Other all-black, similarly equipped people are preparing the truck to be loaded.

The man in the doorway steps softly inside, looking around cautiously for any people or animals, but there is none. The dark figure looks at the control panel, which can only be seen because he has little flashlights on his head. It reads disarmed.

Sitting at his nice modern stone dining table, Mark has an excellent view of his deck and yard. He scans the yard and quickly notices that the landscape seems a bit different from a few weeks ago. Rising from his seat, he grabs his cappuccino and walks to the deck to take a closer look, all in one smooth motion.

Turning as he walks, he notices Mairis cooking breakfast. She looks nearly identical to Alice. He comments to himself that since her makeover, she has been so similar to Alice that he could have sworn it actually is Alice. He has known Alice for years in his dreams and thought he knew Alice well.

Mairis looks directly at Mark as he observes her. "Did you notice my new car? Do you like it?"

Mark, now standing at the glass doors to the deck, smiles. "Ah, it's a classic. The 1997 Lotus Esprit. Yeah, it sizzles."

Mairis smirks with a nearly lottery-winning-bad-girl look as a solitary teardrop streams toward her chin. "I had to sign my life away to get it, but it is most certainly worth every penny thus far."

Mark looks out the window at his yard, returning to his previous objective. The trees are noticeably different. Even the shrubs and grass are different. Mark quickly scans his neighbor's yard to assure himself that he isn't delusional, which still appears the same as previous observations. His grass looks much softer and velvety now.

The trees and shrubbery noticeably swoop in smooth curves, lines, and sharp edges.

Mairis, still tending to the eggs and bacon, continues, "I am going to get a carbon fiber body kit and hood when I can muster up the monies. Don't you think that would look hot?"

Mark smirks while observing his yard. "Good idea. I do that to all my cars."

Mark scans his neighbor's shrubbery again, which still looks prickly and rough despite being nicely cut and detailed.

Mairis looks up at him and says, "I really like how you have designed your domain here. The minimal decor has really extraordinary aesthetics. I would say you need a bit more décor, though."

Mark sips his coffee and looks at her, "Yeah, it sizzles. I am pleased you find it appealing. Obviously, you have good taste—much like me. One of the reasons why I like you."

Stepping back with thoughtfulness, she says, "You'll have to help me design and assemble my domain sometime. I would love that!"

Suddenly noticing that the atmosphere in the room seems warm and inviting with thick-like energy, Mark shifts his eyes and then responds, "Absolutely, we can do that. That seems like a fun way to spend a day."

Mark turns toward the dinette table, observing the plate of food Mairis has placed. Contemplating what he has just observed, he looks around the room. Finally, he thought to himself, it's as if the outside is now reflecting my style here on the inside. It did seem like his style had affected every corner of his yard.

Reaching into his pocket, Mark pulls some cash out of his wallet and places it near Mairis, then whispers, "Body kit and hood."

Mairis slightly leaps and then smiles. "Thank you so much. You are awesome." Calming down a bit, she takes a bite of food while seemingly examining the other side of the room. "I really like your dreams."

Interrupting her, Mairis's tablet announces an incoming call, to which she answers briskly. "Hey, John."

It is Officer John Thomas who immediately responds, "I wanted you to know that Tina has been reported missing. She did not show up for work and was not found at her apartment. We will be investigating it shortly."

Mairis' face turns pale, "Oh, my—." Then she turns silent.

Mark inquisitively quickly finishes a bite and then queries, "What is it?"

Mairis blandly replies, "Tina is missing."

A sudden intensity overcomes Mark, "What! Where was she last?"

Mairis still blandly replies out of shock, "She never returned from her brother's place."

Mairis starts dialing Tina's brother from her tablet.

Mark's face turns to utter determination, "What about her apartment?"

Mairis's face now changes to concern as she begins to come back from wherever that sent her, "We live together, so I would know."

Mark shifts backward, having calmed down a bit but still determined, "Looks like I'm going to need to drive to Tina's brother's house and see if I can find any clues along the way... Do you have his address?"

The automatic garage door is closing behind him; Mark relocates his leather trench coat, allowing him to make a smooth exit from the vehicle. His Acura TLX is gleaming and shining, with only a few minor dusty smudges. Mark had it detailed and washed only a few days ago. The smell of wood and dust wisps around him while he exits into the house.

The sunny, clear blue skies emanate through the large glass windows while Mark turns on his entertainment system. Reaching for his espresso maker, he quickly starts a cup. Mark then tosses some cubed filet mignon, onions, and pepper in a frying pan. Suddenly, the doorbell announces a guest. Mark swiftly maneuvers to the front door.

"Hello, my dear friend, and how are you?" Mark gleefully acknowledges. Standing at the door, resting most of his weight on one leg, Ramses is wearing a shimmering black vinyl jacket with neon-green stripes, a black pinstriped pair of shimmering dress pants, and a shiny green rayon top with a partially unzipped brass zipper.

Ramses removes his designer sunglasses and says, "How is it, my friend!"

Mark, still ecstatic, "Come in. Do you want some filet tips?" They quickly relocate to the den-and-kitchen area, where the filet cubes are still sizzling. Mark finishes the mini filet wraps and brings them to the table.

"Nice yard! I wonder why yours looks so different from all the neighbors?" Ramses facetiously queries.

"Well, you know it's my magic essence," Mark responds, laughing.

Grabbing a wrap, Ramses moves to the large foyer area. "I like the decor you've applied. That is a nice piece. Where did you get that?"

Mark meanders along. "Oh, that is a piece that I hold captive as a loan guarantee. It is my collateral." Ramses chuckles. "Now, you're a lender and a loan shark; what's next, a bank?"

The smooth lines on Ramses' face do not make him appear old. His skin folds in a way that makes his face look chiseled and refined, like a block of stone come to life.

"I'm not sure if I will go as far as becoming a bank. That requires a lot more focus on things I currently employ my bank to do," Mark responds swiftly while still exposing a slight laugh.

"Smart move with the collateral," Ramses says, with one hand at his side while the other one follows his close inspection of the art piece.

Ramses looks at Mark somberly. "My house was burglarized last night."

Chuckling a bit, he continues, "I had no TV, so I came over here to bother you!"

Mark walks to the billiards table and starts up a game, but then stops to pay more attention to the conversation.

Mark looks at him. "Any idea who did it?"

Ramses' eyes look to the side, then down. "No, they left some weird message on my answering machine in some low, raspy whisper-like tone that said something like 'We took what we wanted.' I figured they disguised the voice."

Mark responds, pointing at Ramses, "They might have something to do with the people who tried to rob me. Hopefully, the police will catch on to that."

Ramses shifts, "Someone 'tried' to rob you? What did they do?"

Mark turns a bit more serious, "At the party, someone... I'm not sure what to call it. Anyway, I couldn't see them. Like the message on your machine, it talked to me, and the next morning, several invalid charges showed on my account."

Ramses slightly squints his eyes and has a slight smile while responding, "I actually interrogated one of these guys and pulled out all the stops, but he wouldn't talk. In fact... heh, I have him in the car right now."

Mark's face suddenly turns to surprise, "You... what? You kidnapped someone and brought him to my house?"

"Well, I was going to let him go. You want to see if you can get him to talk?"

Mark, still intensely concerned, "What if the police come over?!"

"Calm down, Mark. If you don't want to talk to him, I'll let him go."

Mark turns to contemplation, "Ughh, yeah, I'll give it a try. I hope you didn't expose too much information. He can go back and tell others."

Ramses exits the house to his car, momentarily returning with Draul, who is bound tightly behind his back with some zip ties. Draul is slightly resistant while Ramses repeatedly pushes him into the room.

Ramses, "Do you have a chair and some rope?"

Mark, "Sure."

Mark pulls up a chair for Draul and then swiftly goes to his garage. Ramses forcefully sits Draul onto the chair and then reaches for the zip ties that Mark has returned with. Zipping the ties, Ramses tightens his legs to the chair.

Mark closely, examining the process, "Easy-easy. We don't need covalent bonds here."

Mark cringed at the sight of a bound man in his house.

Talking purposely in earshot of Draul, Mark says to Ramses, "Okay, we let him go after he speaks."

Ramses smiles at the subtle move by Mark, "That's the idea."

Mark turns to Draul, "Why did you kidnap our friends? Why do you think we aren't real, and what is it that isn't real?"

Draul looks Ramses directly in the eyes and speaks as if he knows a secret, "Why don't you ask Mark why we're here? After all, the portal is his doing."

Much to Draul's delight, Ramses suddenly turns to Mark, "You're why all this is happening?"

Mark, undaunted, continues talking to Draul, "I did what? Why do you think I opened the portal?"

Ramses turns soft and contemplative, looking around as if searching for something, yet not really seeing anything, and lowers his tone, "You're the reason Selene is missing?"

Draul, with a sly smile, says, "I think you know why."

Mark is now irritated; he responds with intensity and determination, "You didn't answer my question. What is the purpose of kidnapping our friends? DON'T YOU WANT US TO LET YOU GO?"

Ramses, snapping out of it, decides he is likely being played, "Give me one piece of evidence that proves Mark opened the portal to your world."

Daul nods his head left and right and sighs a large sigh, "You don't get it; Mark is unique. His reach is impressive; he definitely created the portal."

Ramses, now determined to side with Mark over his criminal captive, defiantly responds, "That doesn't prove anything. I know what you're doing. You're trying to drive a wedge between us. It won't work."

Ramses continues, "Don't you have anything worthwhile to say so we can understand all this nonsense?"

Draul, realizing he cannot divide them, droops his head, then slowly looks back up.

"Okay... okay. Look... they don't know what this place is, but they think it is some sort of virtual dream world or something... ... They are not in charge here.. at least not yet."

Ramses clips the zip ties and unties Draul.

Ramses, "Your friends are mistaken and need to learn how to get along with others; now get out of here!"

Draul feels his hands, and a look of shock comes over his face. He slowly stands up and looks at Mark. With a jolt, he runs for the door and doesn't look back.

Ramses presses his earpiece, "Follow him casually."

Chapter 10

Gone Missing

After driving for several hours, Mark rolls into a small town outside Olympus called Vashon. Nearly all the buildings have boarded or blacked-out windows. Mark reaches Vashon Highway, which seems to be the main road, but Vashon appears to be a ghost town. Turning right, he proceeds south as advised by Tina and, sure enough, reaches Cemetery Road.

At least the Coffee shop on the right is still open. Mark points to the Coffee shop as a mental note to know he can return to it if he needs help finding the tree. Mark notices some old classic piano music. *Is that in my head?* The sound is clear and stark, unlike the usual tunes that play in his mind.

"One more block," He says to himself.

Mark passes more boarded-up buildings, a pizzeria, an auto glass store, and some sizeable buildings. There is another boarded-up building on the left, and he notices that much of the ground next to it is covered in black. So, Mark pulls into the parking area of the boarded-up Estate Sales company.

Suddenly, Mark remembers... A picture of the receipt from Vashon Estate Sales, signed by Thekaf; it is the company from his father's will. The company Thekaf hired to sell anything Mark did not want to keep. Mark parks his car near the apparently abandoned building and exits toward the black grounds near the woods, not too far away.

Reaching the woods, he looks around; everything is covered in this pitch-black, ultra-light material. Oddly, when he steps on it, the ground remains fully covered. He notices a trail into the woods, so he pulls out his flashlight and follows the path. Even in the sunshine, everything seemed so dark.

A short while up the trail, Mark comes upon a Douglas fir tree completely covered in black, but in the tree is a rusty old bicycle. It is inside the tree, the wheels sticking out at both ends. Mark examines the picture, comparing it to the actual one. The bicycle has the same thick tires and all, but it is NOT inside the tree in his picture. He snaps a picture of the tree with a bicycle in it.

"I wonder whose bicycle this was and how did it get in the tree?"

Using his flashlight, Mark walks around the tree. Behind the tree is a crater-like dip in the ground; at the center is a small orb also covered in black. Mark snaps a picture and then picks up the orb, which is a little smaller than the palm of his hand.

Mark rubs the orb to see if he can remove the black film. The black film reluctantly rubs off to reveal that the orb is, in fact, clear. It appears to be glass or crystal. At its center is a tiny, glowing light, reminiscent of a campfire spark.

When suddenly, a low, raspy voice talks to him, "You're too late. Dear old Dad led us right to it."

Mark quickly zaps, "Did father have a portal?"

The raspy voice snarks, "I almost feel sorry for you, you don't know? Daddy abandoned you with his portal to Earth. This is all that remains of it. Are you missing dear old daddy?"

Mark doesn't bother playing the voice's game and instead speaks with authority, "Where's Tina?"

Mark looks around, and then specifically where the voice seems to be coming from, but nothing is to be seen except the same black film that covers the rest of the area.

Raspy voice responds, "She's enjoying a new life."

Mark, "What do you want?"

"You already know from the video game; gift us the sword of Darthor, and we'll leave you alone."

Mark, "Why don't you get it yourself?"

"The sword is just a symbol of your submission."

Mark decides to explore what the terms are of this, "If I do that, could I see my father again?"

The voice laughs, "Daddy's gone, you won't be seeing him again... but you could see Tina again."

Leveling his hands into two fists evenly spaced on each side, he decides to give the voice a sample. Mark fills with intensity deep within and grunts, causing ripples of energy to echo all around him, clearing the immediate black coating near him.

Mark ferociously responds, "Not a chance!"

He presses his ear while exiting the woods and calls Mairis, reaching voicemail.

Mark, "Mairis, calling to check if everything is okay and if there is any status on Tina."

Mark is sitting at his massive computer workstation, examining the screen intently. Sitting next to him is the orb he obtained from the Vashon tree. The orb rests on two curved, soft stands and is littered with electrode and sensor pads wired to a small circuit board. The circuit board is connected to his computer's USB port. He is examining the software used to connect to the electrodes on the computer screen.

Readings are minimal, probably because the tiny spark has since gone out. Mark clicks a button, and two electrodes emit electricity to each other, like positive and negative; it appears like tiny lightning.

"Cool."

Measurements, however, mostly stay the same. Mark adjusts the voltage on his software by turning a dial and then clicks a button again. The whole ball lights up very briefly, but there is still no real change.

Mark finds his way to his silky bed after a brief hot soak. Stopping, he drifts off to the state of mind known as sleep, where he finds himself on a gigantic walking street during a nice sunny day. The cloudless sky makes it feel like there is vast amounts of space available for exploring. Mark suddenly pushes with his legs and leaps into the sky, soaring. As he begins to lose momentum, he pushes again with his hips. Even though there is only air beneath his legs, he can again leap and soar. Mark easily controls his movement by shifting left or right.

Mark soars through the sky for a brief while in this manner when an in-flight falcon suddenly maneuvers into his immediate vicinity. It soars next to him, showing him an unusual curiosity. An odd feeling comes over Mark, as if something is wrong. Looking down, there is a walkway, some beachside houses, and a dark jungle. In the distance, a mountain that seems oddly similar to Mount Zurich. Mark's senses suggest there is something that he knows down there, so he decides to take a closer look.

Mark says to himself, "Isis, where are you?"

Landing, Mark looks around. The sandy beach lacks people, yet there are houses. The atmosphere is warm and inviting until the deep, dark jungle. Mark has odd sensations as though dangerous things are transpiring. He thought, Why don't they come out to the beach where it is warm and inviting? He concludes that exposure wasn't part of the plan. They might be afraid of him and were trying to project fear.

Suddenly, Mark realizes who the person might be. It is Isis, the girl he had met at the party. She might be here somewhere, according to his senses. Mark kneels and places his hand out toward the ground.

A large spider emerges from under his shirt sleeve. Mark instructs it, "Go and locate Isis."

He makes a brief sweep of the area and then decides to visit her place instead. Suddenly, the Falcon swoops down and picks up the spider that appears to have been awaiting the bird on the ground. Mark turns and leaps into the air to visit Isis's place when suddenly, there is a loud noise.

Mark opens his eyes to the usual ceiling patterns and reaches for the "noise" that is, in fact, his alarm.

On his way back from work, Mark opens the door, stepping out into the parking lot, where he locates his Acura across the lot through the drenching downpour. Raindrops forcefully assault his exposed hands until Mark fits his black leather gloves. Navigating his leather trench coat, Mark makes his way to the driver's seat. Pulling out his tablet, he quickly zaps a text before igniting the engine.

Reaching his house, Mark quickly sautés some vegetables and chicken strips while watching the current previews of upcoming movies.

"There you are," a raspy voice says, causing Mark to jitter out of surprise, slightly spilling his espresso.

The voice continues, "Your friend Ramses has some nice things. He should keep them better guarded. Not to worry, I'll be leaving. I had the displeasure of meeting your friendly pet spiders."

Mark thought to himself, What the? My spiders? Ha, hopefully, they beat the crap out of him.

Mark then responds, "Ramses was probably not expecting thieves to visit while he was out. I am sure you would be the one surprised next time around."

There is no response to Mark's retort. Mark intently scrutinizes the room, especially where it seems the voice was coming from. Possibly, it was on the other side of the crème-colored wall, and Mark could find nothing to indicate anything unusual. However, he did find new satisfaction in the wall pattern, which has a lightly painted green gradient grid pattern in a sort of curved three-dimensional fashion, overlaying the crème wall. Mark returns and swiftly finishes his espresso.

Escaping to his car in the garage, Mark zips out into the heavy rain. Hugging the curves, Mark accelerates a bit above the speed limit. The windshield wipers made a slight yet swift, sweeping, and zipping noise with seemingly endless attempts to keep the window free of liquid rain. Turning to his tablet, he hits the redial, only to again get Isis's machine. Mark cannot help but wonder if Isis is well and why she did not answer her phone.

Intently observing the road ahead, Mark suddenly has a sense of déjà vu. Mark slows down to carefully analyze a small dirt road that exits from the main road. There is something eerily familiar about it. Deciding it would only take a minute, he turns onto the small dirt road.

A revelation overcomes Mark as he comments to himself, "No! Really? Th--this is th-e road?"

The road appears nearly identical to the one he frequently visits in his dreams. While he came in slightly different from his dream travels, it clearly either is its twin or it is, in fact, the road. For some reason, Mark had thought the road was simply a dreamscape invention and not an actual road he could locate. Finally, Mark decides he had better finish checking on Isis, and he could explore the road later.

Arriving at her apartment, Mark quickly recognizes her beautiful i8 Spider. He looks through a few windows on the vehicle, but nothing appears out of the ordinary. He examines the tires and ensures nothing around the car is unusual. Mark scans the parking lot carefully, but all looks normal, so he strolls observantly to the townhouse.

He knocks on the townhome door for a while; there is seemingly no response. Turning to the nearby neighbor's door, he knocks.

A woman answers in her robe, "Hello, can I help you?"

Mark, "Have you seen your neighbor, Isis, in the past few days?"

The large-sized woman continues dismissively, waving her hands, "No, I seldom see her. I don't know what her schedule is."

Mark, undaunted, continues to query, "Okay, have you noticed anything unusual about that apartment recently?"

The woman touches her face with her index finger, and her expression turns to thoughtfulness, "Only a man has been visiting her lately. I think it's her brother. What was unusual was that he was talking to someone even though he was alone."

Mark's eyes shift, looking around and in thought before returning to the woman, "Mmm. Any idea what he was saying?"

Squinting her eyes slightly, the woman continues, "Not sure; it was something about doing something for someone... It didn't make a lot of sense."

Mark smiles and decides to investigate the apartment further, "Thanks."

Slipping around the back, Mark thought about the oddity of a growling black, almost sickly hyena with long, scraggly, straight hair and striped legs in a distant, large, open field.

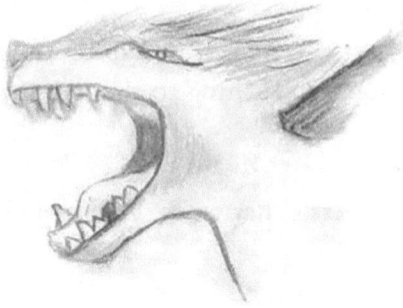

He browses the large glass back doors. Isis' place is nearly empty, with only the largest items remaining. Even more strange is that they are chaotically lying around.

"She did not say anything about moving," Mark thought while calling the police station.

The rain has subsided by the time John Thomas arrives on the scene, "Hello, Mark. How well did you know Isis? I'll need a statement."

Mark smirks, "Well enough. I think she would have told me if she were moving. I tried to call her all day. After there was no answer, I came out here to discover her townhouse in disarray. Do you need anything from me? Now that you are here, I figure on letting you do your job."

John looks him up and down with thoughtfulness. "All I need to know is the last time she contacted you. Then we can investigate the scene, and you can go."

Slightly looking up yet not really "looking," Mark ponders that, "The... the last time... was two days ago. She called me on my tablet to see what was up and if I would have another party. I told her that due to some strange thefts, I would not be having any parties for now and that I would let her know."

John quickly jots some things down. "You tried to call her, and it was suspicious that she was not answering 'all day,' prompting you to drive out here and discover her townhouse apparently in disarray while her car was still here. Correct?"

Mark says with a serious look, "Yes. I did not go inside. I merely observed from the windows."

John closes his tablet computer cover to prevent the rain from touching the screen, "Great! Thank you, you may go."

While returning, Mark decides to stop at the road he had noticed on his way to Isis's apartment. Turning off the main road, it is a small dirt road. After a short while, the trail turns dusty; he slows and rolls to a stop.

Looking around, it is still light outside, and he can view the landscape with ease. Mark carefully examines his slightly shaking hand and realizes he is unsure of what might be here, something he may be unable to see while in a waking state. Hidden entities that may be only visible from the dream state.

The short, weedy grass is blowing lightly in the breeze. An exceptional view of the horizon reminds him he has a few hours left of daylight. Mark exits his vehicle and closes the door softly as if this is some momentous occasion. Scanning the scene, it looks sort of like his dream.

Mark begins walking the dusty trail, and he feels it is almost identical to the dreams he experienced as he walked the road. After a short while, he can see a lone, solitary tree with vibrant green leaves. Mark mutters to himself while intently scrutinizing every detail of what his visual cortex is displaying to his mind.

"Is... that the tree?! It must be. It looks like it."

A slight breeze delivers a wisp of dust and grass in the otherwise clean-smelling air. It is almost as if something is responding to his discovery. Mark turns and examines the travel path that he had momentarily walked. The grass appears to whisk circularly with the breeze as if somehow pointing to his trail.

An old shoe is resting a few inches away from where he had walked. The old shoe suddenly gives him a strong feeling of déjà vu, as if it were somehow an old friend. Mark mumbles as he retraces his steps. He approaches the shoe and then stoops down to examine it more closely. Inside the shoe is a décor item. It is the symbol of an eye. Mark pulls the eye out of the shoe and looks it over.

"Thank you, old friend. Now I know the dreams are real." He decides it is time to return home and makes his way to his car.

Walking around the car, John carefully analyzes every detail. The fingerprint duster is still delicately at work on the inside. Looking back, John can still see Tina's dead corpse en route to the coroner's and almost in the ambulance. The flashing turn signal light is particularly annoying when it's combined with the windshield wipers.

"Turn those things off as soon as you can, please," The fingerprint duster, who is putting everything away, quickly reaches over and shuts the car off.

Softly approaching, Thoth announces, "So what do we have thus far?"

John zaps back, "No fingerprints except the victim. It's like the car suddenly just drove off the road."

Thoth responds in a matter-of-fact tone, "The body has been here for a while, several hours at least. No houses nearby, and anyone driving by would likely have thought little of it."

John shows a bit of surprise, "Really, and the car was 'on' the whole time? I wonder if there was someone else who drove her here."

John carefully examines the car seats. "Well, there is no evidence to prove another person was in the car. However, we cannot rule it out."

Thoth interjects, "Well, another mysterious event. Did you check for more of that aluminum oxide material?"

John turns toward Thoth, "Why yes, there does appear to be a small amount of it over here near the wheel. They may utilize it to coat or protect something." John points to the steering wheel.

"I cannot believe there is no evidence of another party being present. I am just glad it isn't... I mean, it could have been worse," Thoth stammers.

"Worse? What could be worse than a beautiful girl and a local citizen dead in such a way?" John's intensity is very sharp.

Thoth, "You're right. I hope this doesn't mean Rae is deceased somewhere."

John, "He would need to be better hidden."

Chapter 11

Dueling Forces

It is a wet one outside, and Mark makes a run for the car. Brushing off the wet, He gets comfortable in his Acura and begins driving when, suddenly, his tablet announces that someone is calling. Answering, Mark is a bit surprised that the police have video on the phone, yet there he is, Officer John Thomas.

"I am calling to let you know that Isis is now a missing person. We won't officially announce it for at least five days from the incident in case she is not a missing person at all, primarily because she called into work. That is the shortest timeframe I can do, you understand? Since her car is still at her apartment and there were signs of odd, possibly chaotic, activity inside, the evidence suggests she was possibly abducted, which is how we came up with the five-day timetable. I did some preliminary research on her whereabouts and came up empty."

Mark frowns. "Not good; she could be in danger during those five days. Thanks for letting me know, anyway."

John continues, "If you come upon any information concerning her whereabouts, make sure you let us know ASAP."

Mark is concerned yet glad to be in the loop. "Will do, thank you."

"Where are you, Isis?" Mark thinks to himself as he races for his dry garage.

Walking through the doorway, Mark notices his tablet alerting him to a text.

The text reads, "Whazzup? Can I come over? I need to come over."

It is Mairis, and Mark texts back, "Sure thing, see you in a bit."

Very shortly, another text shows. "Sifive, Mark. I am here at Ramses' place, helping him secure his place after the burglary. Did you want to hang out at Ramses' place?" This time, it is Garrick with the sifive hello, which is their version of a high-five hello.

Mark texts back, "Well, Mairis is coming over, so perhaps another time. So, apparently, Isis is a missing person, according to Officer John. However, he cannot pursue Isis too much until after five days have passed so as to make it official."

Garrick responds with a frown. "Bum deal, I'll keep an eye out."

Garrick continues, "I visited Dacian's house to see if I could see or hear anything obvious about it, and I came up with nothing. There seems to be nothing unusual about it or the area. I did discover that Chris Vocal is also blind and the owner of the company. On the other hand, I had an encounter with one of our vocal friends."

Mark texts back, "Really, what happened? I mean, what did the so-called voice say?"

Garrick responds, "Well, it told me to keep to my own business and would not comment about any thefts. The thing slightly threatened me if I get a little too nosy."

Garrick continues, "Can you believe the audacity of that? I should mind my own business! Perhaps if they didn't attack people we care about. I could have picked it up at Ramses' place, the Cyberpad, Dacian's, or somewhere between."

Mark makes a smirking smiley face, "Well, that narrows it down. It could have been any of those places. If it had something to do with Ramses' robbery, it may have been there. On the other hand, it could be saying that because you were checking out Dacian's place."

Garrick responds, "I also plan on paying a visit to Chris Vocal's abode. I'll let you know how it goes."

Staring at the object, Mairis comments, "This is a fascinating piece. Where did you get this?"

Mark, with two drinks in hand, says, "It is collateral for a loan. If or when Josh can pay me what is owed, then I'll return the captive art to him."

Again, Mark notices that Mairis looks like Alice to the point that she is almost indistinguishable from Alice. Mairis carefully examines the protruding jungle tree elements of the three-dimensional object. It is primarily a painted object that appears as a sort of three-dimensional passageway to a wild jungle region. The painted imagery also has three dimensions, giving the illusion of an actual passageway. The detail is a bit rough, which was probably done on purpose, yet it seems eerily real, as if there actually is a way to step through it and into the wild jungle.

"So sad about Tina." Mairis softly held Mark's hand.

"I can't believe she is dead; my mind hasn't fully processed it," Mark reacts to the reference to Tina.

Mairis looks longingly into Mark's eyes, "This is scary... Don't you fear that one of us could be next?"

Mark reaches forward, hugging and consoling her.

He responds in kind and continues, "We'll find 'em... We'll find 'em."

Mairis cries a little uncontrollably, her makeup streaming down her face. Mark consoles her, and she settles down a bit. Mairis, tears in her eyes, turns her head into Mark's embrace.

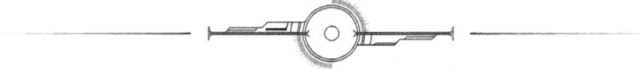

Mark's dream at the nearby dirt road.

Mark is standing on the grassy plain near the usual dusty road. In his hand, the orb from the Vashon bicycle tree. Placing it on a small stand in front of him, he checks the rubber feet that keep it from rolling. Mark scans the area, but nobody is nearby, and the faint breeze is pleasant.

Turning back toward the orb, Mark focuses his eyes, and a hot, forceful luminate wave emits from them, hitting the orb. After a moment, Mark stops to observe the orb; the faint spark at the center of the orb is back. Mark hits the orb again with another wave, and the spark grows even bigger. Touching the orb, Mark discovers it is scorching to the touch:

"Ouch!"

Again, Mark hits it with a wave. This time, the orb illuminates, but the rubber feet melt, and the stand collapses under some unknown exaggerated weight. The illuminated orb has burned a hole in the stand and now rests glowing in the burnt grass. Reaching down, Mark touches the orb, but it is no longer too hot to touch. He picks it up and places it in his pocket.

Present-day Braila

Awakening, Tina groggily and slowly opens her eyes. Looking around, Tina is lying in a large, slightly comfortable bed. Still half awake, she rolls around comfortably and sighs.

"Wait...," she thought to herself.

As she reaches to free herself from the down comforter, she immediately notices her hands are different. They look much younger than she expected. She looks up and down her hands and arms. Quickly locating a mirror across the room, she peers into the reflection with awe. Had she somehow found a time machine or grown younger? She looks like she did when she was in her early teenage years. She is still like herself, only around ten years younger.

"Whoa!" she announces out loud.

Looking around the dainty room, it is full of frills and pastels: small items, decor mixed with modern yet still older things. The room is like something she might have had at such an age, yet never remembers living in.

Suddenly, from a dark corner, a raspy voice says, "Welcome to your new home, Tina, or shall we call you Jara?"

Carefully, Tina looks at the corner, seeing nothing; she walks to the only door in the room. She looks up at the door as she reaches for the handle. Opening the door, she peers on the other side.

"Jara, honey, breakfast is ready." Announces an elder female voice, possibly her mother. Tina thought to herself again, Where the heck am I?

Reaching for the door, Mark thinks to himself, at least it isn't raining today. The overcast sky looms, yet the cumuli are not quite as dark as yesterday, providing a glimmer of blue sky. Mark quickly locates his desk and is loading the CAD software when his messenger starts alerting him. It is Tink.

"Hey, can I visit? It's my break, and I tire of sitting at my desk." Tink has an earlier shift that he selected by choice.

Mark quickly zaps back. "Sure, you know where my desk is, correct?"

Turning his head, Mark notices Jaul at his door. "What's up, Jaul?"

Jaul smiles. "How are you doing? Familiarizing yourself with everything?"

Mark responds, "So far so good, it's Tink's break. Is it okay if he visits for a bit?"

Jaul zaps back. "Sure, no problems. This is a comfortable environment if you haven't noticed. As long as you are getting the work done."

Mark smirks, pleased with the response. "So how is biz? Everything okay on the improving sales front?"

Jaul looks slightly to the side, his eyes shift, and he slightly frowns. "Well, actually, those sales are costing us more money than anticipated. Sales are up, yet so are costs. So, it is a bit up in the air right now on how it will go."

Mark, tapping his pen, shows a serious look. "Okay, let me know if there is something I can do. I'll be working on the new sensor tech as requested for now."

Jaul smiles widely; his body movement goes with the smile, and it appears to be the answer he was looking for. "Sure, thank you, and I'll let you know."

Tink slips past Jaul in the doorway with a minor acknowledgment of each other. Mark, observing the encounter, smiles at Tink.

"Whazzup! Tink!"

Tink with a slight smug smile, handing Mark a clear plastic bottle. "Would you like bottled water?"

Mark nods his head. "Thanks."

Tink makes himself comfortable on the edge of the desk and looks at Mark. His long dark hair is slightly shorter now. "So, how do you like this versus designing video games?"

Mark, fixing his wavy yet short auburn hair as a sort of auto-reflex, responds, "I'm not sure yet. Designing video games was quite fun, but this tool will also be used to explore and detect the unknown, which I find interesting. The video game design is a bit more creative."

Tink smiles quickly, sips his water, and then moves his hair out of his face. He touches his head briefly and continues, "Why did you make those things up in your video games? I mean, in the last video game you designed, a city called Olympia of the Pacific Northwest, rather than the real city of Olympus on Lake Victoria. There were some similarities, but it was nearly always rainy, and the area seemed to have too many evergreen trees around. Why lie like that? Why not simply call it Olympus? More like the real thing we live with?"

Mark laughs, shaking his entire chair slightly. "Well, it needed to be like the player is reaching into another dimension yet feel like they've been somewhere similar, at least for that game. For the maps, it wasn't all about being creative; it was meant to be a slightly familiar world."

Tink continues, "What about the people who don't live in Olympus? If they look up Olympia, they may not find Olympus."

Mark still smirks. "It is a real place, like another thread to the multiverse. They step into the video game and explore a real virtual world with cities like an alternate version. It is not meant to be an exact replica of the cities in our world."

Pausing, Mark continues, "'Do,' you must know, you've played the game. Didn't you like exploring the game universe that I designed?"

Tink starts laughing and looks him in the eye after chugging on his water, "I'm just messing with you, "do." I know it's another world for the gamer to explore. Have you ever thought from a different perspective like that?"

Mark, relieved, relaxes his arms on his chair. "Ha! Very funny, but no. It has crossed my mind, but they are real places to me."

What a conversation. Was he simply trying to have fun, or were there subtle hints suggesting that what I did before wasn't real? Good luck with that one.

Mark continues, "Tink, don't let this place get to you, 'do.'"

Tink laughs it off, "Well, I had an epiphany the other day and was thinking about our previous work. I had to discuss it with someone. I'd better get back to work. Talk later, 'do.'"

Mark continues analyzing the schematics of the underwater sea vehicle; it only slightly varies from the space version of the vehicle. The objective was to ensure the maximum effectiveness of the sensors and capabilities in as many situations as possible. The initial sensor is obvious; make room and place one inside the vehicle's drill. This way, it could take measurements of the area around the drill target. Often, the objective is to see, hear, touch, or otherwise detect things that are difficult to see. He spent the rest of the day examining various possible positions.

Approaching his house, Mark notices the oddity of a solitary white lark with black wings standing in the center of his walkway. Parking his car in his garage, Mark slips in via the garage doorway to his house.

Swiftly grabbing a scoop of coffee, Mark starts a cup of espresso. Mark's tablet suddenly alerts him of a call, and he quickly grabs it.

"Mark here," He knew it wasn't Garrick because of the generic ringtone.

A picture of Josh comes into view. "Hey, Mark. What's up!"

Mark smiles while wiping his hands. "Josh, how are you on this fine day?"

Mark reaches over and turns on his computerized TV system.

Josh then continues, "Guess what? I have your three hundred thousand credits."

Mark, now excited yet also a little disappointed, says, "Awesome. I really liked your art and will regret seeing it go. However, the 300K will come in handy. When do you want to arrange for the exchange?"

Josh chuckles. "Can I pick it up today?"

Mark responds, "Sure, as long as I can verify funds. I'll be here the rest of the day."

"I'll make the transfer now," Josh states with a smile and swiftly ends the call.

A mere 10 minutes have passed, with Mark comfortably sipping his espresso while watching the news, before Mark's door alarm announces. Mark grabs his tablet and casually makes his way toward the door, his senses tingling with satisfaction as he navigates the thick atmosphere of his home.

Reaching the door, Mark recognizes Josh. "So, you finally mustered the credits, huh?"

Josh made a broad smile while fidgeting with his shirt. "Yes. Yes. Did you confirm the funds?"

Mark smiles with confidence as he smoothly waves his arm, indicating that Josh come in, "Not yet, let me do that."

Quickly tapping his tablet a few times, Mark pulls up the transaction, and it shows completed with a confirmation number. Immediately behind Josh are two workmen dressed all in white and holding a container. The men walk towards the sizeable three-dimensional art piece and begin preparing the container for transport.

Josh, "I nearly thought I wouldn't need to pay this, but Sett and crew didn't grab it."

Mark's facial expression turns from pleasant to shock as he stops in his tracks, "What?"

After a short pause, Mark continues, "Is Sett in town?"

Josh is suddenly unsure. He wasn't aware that Mark didn't know Sett was in the area.

Josh says, "He hangs out with some people in remote areas."

Mark, now a little unnerved, but coming back around, "That conniving bastard shouldn't have come to Olympus. Do you know why he's here?"

Josh puts his hands up, waving them in a non-aggressive manner, "No idea. I've never been to his place; that's all I know."

Mark was a little disturbed that Josh didn't tell him anything about this, "You could have warned me."

Josh, now a little defensive, "And risk my life? I prefer not to get involved."

Josh turns, looking at the painting, "It is in excellent condition and looks even better than the day I let you hold it."

Mark returns to smiles, "I had it touched up. Well, it was in the middle of my main foyer."

Josh laughs as he exits immediately behind the movers. "Alright, thanks again."

Mark waits for Josh to leave, then quickly reaches for his earpiece, placing a call, "I need to speak to John Thomas or someone working the Isis case."

After a long day, Mark is glad to have an extra three hundred thousand credits, and he makes his way to his large, comfortable bed. Soon, Mark shifts into sleep, finding himself in the field he had frequently visited.

Mark walks along the dirt road; he notices the oddity of two bright blue frogs with slightly hunched backs on the side of the road. He thought he should put some feelers out to find Tina. A short distance away, several people appeared to be running to and fro around a partially luminous and partially black cloud. They are utilizing what appears to be nets and highly reflective tools such as mirrored shovels.

A sticky, large, thick black liquid begins oozing out of the cloud. In the distance, a large dam holds back an unknown amount of water. A small leak in the dam is allowing water to turn what was a dry riverbed into a small stream.

Mark looked again at the cloud and thought, "I hope this doesn't have anything to do with Tina." Immediately, nearby men grab several large, flat, mirrored shovels and begin shoveling the liquid back into the cloud as much as possible.

A large black figure rises out of the liquid; even its eyes are black. Leaping towards the figure, Mark focuses his eyes, which emanate thick, hot, forceful waves. The black figure withstood several blows from the waves, which obviously affected it, but then it responded by forcing Mark to the ground.

Landing on the ground, Mark steadies himself and swings his fist at the dark figure. The dark figure catches the punch with its hand, which immediately turns into liquid black goo surrounding Mark's fist. The black figure smiles at Mark's attempt to punch him.

Mark again focuses his eyes, which emanate thick, hot, forceful waves blasting the dark figure like a strong wind. The dark figure slightly backs up at that. Having a little space, Mark gets up and crouches. Then he slams his fist onto the ground, causing energy waves to echo in all directions. The black figure loses its balance from the waves.

Shortly, the black figure returns to a liquid and unsteadily makes a zigzagging stream toward Mark. Suddenly, Mark can hear Tina from the direction of the cloud.

Tina, "Mark, don't worry. I like it better here. I wish you well, but I've moved on."

Mark is a little off-balance from the interruption from Tina, "Tina? Y... you're alive?"

Mark exerts himself, reaching for Tina. Stretching, and stretching some more.

"Uggghhh!"

In front of him, a bright portal or sphere fades into view. There Tina is, shimmering brightly, except she looks like a young child or teenager.

Mark, "T... Tina? Is that really you?"

It is Tina, she is still conscious! Mark looks around. She's mo-ved on? Sh-sh-e c-an-t... That can't really be her, can it? Mark reaches out for what seems like Tina. Quick before she's gone. He reaches harder and harder. He somehow stretches and reaches further and further; she seems to shimmer brightly. It appeared as if he was stretching for hours until he could al-mo-st gr-asp it, w-was it her? She suddenly vanishes.

The men digging with the shovels intercept the zigzagging black liquid and begin tossing it toward the portal. Mark chuckles; I guess thick liquid wasn't the best choice at the moment.

Mark opens his eyes with force to the usual patterns on the ceiling.

"Dammit!" Mark intensely clenched his fists while yelling with ferocity.

Chapter 12

The Returning

That night, Garrick is investigating addresses found by Mark in his previous dream.

Garrick is driving down a main road northwest of Olympus. The moonlight is vibrant and differs from the warm yellowish light of the street lights. This part of town is upper class, with finely crafted yards, but the roads are mostly dirt or gravel. A place where wealthy people can find privacy and a lot of land.

He reaches a small dirt road near Chris Vocal's house, which is on the other side of the shrubbery and foliage. Garrick parks out of the way behind some of the foliage to remain unseen. Pausing, he checks his gear to ensure he has everything. Garrick exits the car quietly. He holds his bag to keep it firm as he slips through the foliage.

Garrick cautiously approaches the lining of bushes and trees that surround the open plane. A small dirt road led to a large, neatly enclosed rock-covered space obviously utilized for parking. A short distance away is an unusually tall and elaborate building with a pastel blue exterior. The building appears to be possibly five stories high, six if one counts the attic area. Not only was it tall, but it seemed to spread for quite a distance.

"This place is massive," Garrick mumbles to himself.

Crawling through the bushes, he can see lights coming from inside. "A blind man who needs lights? He must have visitors, caretakers, or something."

He slowly makes his way across the open space in the most subtle way he can. The vibes coming from the environment are very unusual. Garrick's extremely perceptive senses are still trying to understand what it is that he is picking up on. It feels as though something is out of place, either him or the building. Not only that, but space seems stretched as if it is distorted.

"Very odd," he mutters to himself.

Reaching the side wall of the large mansion, Garrick notices an unusually dark black corner. He approaches the corner, which now appears nearly unnaturally "black." Garrick then scans the area; nobody seems to be within viewing range.

Reaching into his satchel, Garrick locates a small gun-like "tool." Steadily, he aims at the corner and presses a button on it. A spread of high-charged ionic particles illuminates every crevice of the corner.

"This light 'gun' is awesome," he thought to himself.

Surprisingly, the black briefly withstood and continued to cover the space. Slowly, the dark covering bursts into little "lit" particles before dissipating. Garrick pulls out a plastic baggy and tweezers. Turning the light gun on low, he looks around and extracts some of the black material.

"Well, it did not speak, say anything, or even make noise, so it must not have been one of our odd intruders. Could it be some sort of camouflage material?"

Garrick decides to make a swift exit due to a significant increase in noise coming from inside the house. He intends to avoid being "found out" in the event that someone could somehow detect what he had momentarily done. Despite the unusual vibes, his senses didn't really prove anything. The freshly discovered black material is a good 'possible' connection to the intruders.

Garrick slips away into the coverage of the trees and extends a little spyglass. He watches from a distance for a while; nothing can be discerned. Removing to his vehicle, he slowly drives away. His senses at maximum alert, Garrick notices that the neighbor's house is entirely black. He almost can't see it and must have missed it on his approach.

He thinks to himself, "This must be the nearby address on the address list."

Garrick slowly rolls to a nicely shaded spot. He scans the house with his spyglass for what seems like an eternity. The house isn't in the same lot as Chris's, but it is suspiciously less than a block away. There appeared to be no lights in the house, but that didn't mean it was vacant.

Garrick slowly crawls up to the wall of the house, which appears to be the side wall. The entire house appears unnaturally black, with several extremely dark crevices. What is inside? As silently as possible, he crouches along the side, peering around the corner. There, he can see the protruding doorway; it is so dark there could be anything within, and he likely wouldn't see it until it is too late. Reaching out, he ensures his light gun functions correctly on a tiny spot just out of view of the doorway.

Ever so slowly, he creeps toward the doorway, pausing multiple times to ensure that if something detects him, they might reveal that fact to him. Every step amplifies the tiniest of noises coming from the ground as he steps on the soft grass carpet. The dark doorway remains as still and silent as ever. Even the grass is blacker than black here; what is this coating that is on everything?

Finally, he reaches the doorway, and the door is open, but there is another solid black door inside. Is that the screen door? If it is a screen door, anyone inside could likely hear and possibly see him. He grips the light gun in his left hand fiercely as he reaches for the handle. As quietly as possible, he turns the handle very slowly, opening the door. To his dismay, he cannot see anything inside. The black coating appears to have covered everything. Garrick steps to the side for a moment, ensuring he is out of view from the door. Drops of sweat drip off the edge of his chin.

What is he going to do? He could use the light gun, which would likely alert anything inside the house, or he could enter the darkness. The only thing he can do is use the light gun, he decides, and then prepares himself for what he is about to do. Before he can do that, he notices footprints in the yard.

Someone else is almost certainly inside; the footprints lead right to the door and vanish. He even utilizes his spyglass on the footprints because it has low-light visibility, which unfortunately didn't work on the house. The footprints appear elongated; the person walking didn't do a good job of picking up their feet.

Aiming the light gun directly at the floor, Garrick presses the trigger. The light particles begin to rip through the black coating, revealing a girl lying on the floor.

With a sigh, "It's Selene!" he whispers. Garrick reaches down, touches Selene, and carefully tries to get her attention. Selene is unresponsive and unconscious.

Garrick softly steps toward her and briskly picks her up.

"Selene, I'm here to help," he stammers, completely failing to remain quiet.

With a jolt, a very large growl accompanied by a bark comes from the utter blackness. Garrick stumbles out of shock, "Shit!"

This is it, is it... game over? He struggles to regain himself. The animal moves around, scraping on some unknown surfaces. He suddenly realizes the animal is still in the darkness. Is it caged?

"Damn, dog's gonna' alert the neighborhood"

Grabbing Selene, Garrick moves as quickly as possible toward his car. Selene is still unconscious and very heavy. The dog barks only a few times. His senses are on high alert as he approaches the car, but there is no other movement. This time, he makes as little noise as possible as he rolls down the small road.

Reaching for his tablet, he places a call, "Yeah, Ramses? I have something for you."

The smell of the forest is well known to forest ranger Anthony Rossi. The air breezes swiftly by his nostrils, satisfyingly fresh and crisp. The wooded landscape is on a slope, and the forest goes as far as Anthony can see. Anthony found the view an improvement over the Ranger Station he had recently come from. Not that the view was that bad, but here he was a lot higher than 948 feet.

"Such a large area, can't magin' how we're supposed to find thieves out here."

Reaching with his right hand, he single-handedly grasps the Meconi's sub sandwich he is enjoying. The sky and atmosphere are warm and sunny, which seems to be noticed by most of the wildlife as well. Anthony has a sample in his portable contaminant detector setup on his truck's flatbed. Setting his sandwich down on his pickup, he marks the location on his tablet to note that he has checked for contamination levels. It is clean and beautiful, as usual.

An odd shift in the wind causes Anthony to look up. "That was cold; how strange," he said to himself.

Grabbing his binoculars, he scans the area. In the distance, the sky is nearly black with something; what is it? Anthony is now intrigued by uncertainty. He monitors it for a moment and realizes it is a pack of Falcons.

"That's even more strange, don't think I've ever seen Falcon's fly like that," Talking to 'himself' out in the wilderness was not unusual. Whom else would he talk to?

Anthony swiftly closes the case on the contaminant detector and closes the truck flatbed. Quickly starting up, he speeds toward the sighting. The off-road pickup breezes quickly through the forest to the vicinity. As he approaches, Tony slows to maintain a bit more stealth out of caution; anything could be occurring. Easier to hide out here, he thought to himself.

Tony slows to a crawl, and then he grabs his binoculars to take a closer look at what he is seeing. He can see two large, all-white moving-style trucks. Several men are apparently loading or unloading the vehicle with a large quantity of what appeared to be used effects. There are also several partially camouflaged buildings and other vehicles nearby.

"I'd better call it."

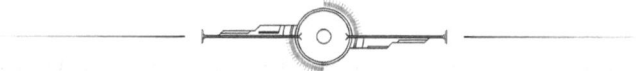

Officer John Thomas has the helicopter land far enough away so as not to draw suspicion and is immediately escorted in a black SUV to the prep site. Arriving, John enters the portable conference trailer.

"What do you have for me?" He queries the local officer in charge.

"With all the thefts going on around, we thought we had better check it out. We did notice some aluminum oxide on the road to this location. They also have all-white moving trucks.

However, electronic equipment, such as tablets, must be turned off because we cannot detect any signals. We do require probable cause to proceed."

John responds, "This seems like the perfect place to hide out, being far enough away from Zurich Route 8143 to the highest point, which likely has too much traffic."

John quickly taps his tablet a few times. After a few moments, he announces, "I have located a signal."

The officer's jaw drops, "How did you do that? We have been scanning for hours."

John casually explains, "Some tablets have an anti-theft device. When the tablet is shut off, it sends a weak, short-range signal on a specific frequency. The signals are powered by an internal battery intended to last a long time. These guys may have anticipated that possibility and figured the remote vicinity prevents detection. Since we are nearby, I was able to pick it up."

John smirks, then continues, "Let's see if we can ID this one. Nice! It is one of the missing persons; Rae's and Isis' tablets are both present. No guarantee anyone is alive, however."

John quickly looks around and then back to Thoth, "Get ready to move."

They spread out as much as possible and cover the only road in and out.

Finally, he announces over a loudspeaker, "Place your hands where we can see them. You are all under arrest!"

Sett is caught off guard by the announcement and immediately ducks behind a truck.

He yells, "Come and take me!"

Sett's men start firing at anyone visible. The sheer quantity of bullets is intense. Suddenly, a large boom erupts, and the scene quickly transforms into a war zone. The boom is a bomb. John flinches as dust and debris scatter everywhere.

The police return fire, and John announces, "We have you surrounded. Put down your weapons and come out with your hands where we can see them."

With that, another barrage of bullets fly through the air, seemingly from everywhere. The dust becomes thick and hard to see as several additional loud booms can be heard near police officer holdouts. John can hear officers helping injured officers escape towards the medical trailer, as well as new officers entering the fight. John continues firing and reloading; a little unsure of exactly what he is firing at, he fires in the general direction of Sett's gang.

The debris is settling, and it is evident that there are a lot fewer bullets in the air. Most of Sett's men are surrendering, while others make a run for it. John and the police advance on their position and begin arresting the perpetrators. John cautiously maneuvers around the truck with his weapon drawn when suddenly a bullet shreds through his right hand, causing him to drop his weapon.

John winces in pain and races for cover. Looking around the corner, it is Sett himself, and he is apparently an excellent shot.

Sett fires again, hitting John in the leg, and says, "They gave me their electronics."

John, wincing in pain, responds, "Then why fight if you will be exonerated?"

Several officers try to find a good place to position themselves.

Suddenly, a massive pulse wave of some sort echoes from Sett's position; a black film swiftly overtakes the truck and the ground.

A scream comes from one of the officers' positions, "Ah-aaah, He-lp." Thoth jolts to the area to assist the officer. A black film begins covering the spot when it abruptly halts.

"Dammit," Sett screams.

John laughs, "What, are you out of mojo, Sett? That's the best you got?"

Several clicking noises come from Sett's gun; He is out of ammo as well. Quickly, he tries to reach for more. Enduring the pain, John jolts toward Sett and grabs onto his arm. Sett reaches around, slamming on John's lower thigh where the bullet wound is. John stammers yet endures and tries to slam him against the truck with all his body weight. Sett twists under the pressure, making a small plea at the pain of his twisted leg and, at the same time, landing John on the ground. John reaches out, grabs Sett's twisted leg, and pulls, causing Sett to fall to the ground. Sett immediately reaches for the ammunition, but it is too late. Several officers surround him with weapons drawn.

Thoth zaps confidently, "Go for it, bud. Give us the satisfaction of gunning you down."

Akutra-Ramses Atenosis Cea

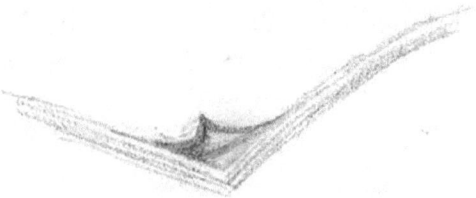

Mark clicks his remote, and his car announces that his alarm is active as he reaches for the office door. Mark has spent the last few days positioning various sorts of sensors optimally and is nearly ready for a prototype. The work is quite tedious, and he had to consider anything that could go wrong, as well as the mathematics of various situations. The drill alone would detect the material composition density of the surrounding soil and even try to see up to one hundred meters.

Mark returns to his desk when Dacian approaches. He turns, facing Dacian.

"Hello, Mark, how are you?"

Mark smirks, "Doing well. I am about to request a prototype, actually."

With a serious look and slightly shifty eyes, Dacian continues, "That is great. We may not be ready to ship the next model, but I'm working on it."

Mark turns serious. "Let me know if there is anything I can do to help. I will continue to do my job until told otherwise." Mark then smirks and continues, "Or you fail to pay my paychecks…"

Dacian smiles nonchalantly. "Okay, no problem. I'll let you know if there are any changes to your position."

Mark continues to his desk and removes his jacket. Mark sits down and sips his coffee before submitting his CAD file to the prototype printer. The prototypes are supposed to be quite remarkably similar to the real thing, but with printed materials. He'll need to assemble it, which allows him to place real sensors for testing purposes. He pulls up the design tools to work on the task when Jaul enters.

Jaul, with a serious look, says, "Mark, is now a good time to talk?"

Mark turns toward Jaul, "As good a time as any."

Jaul continues, "We know you have been asking Tink to look around, Mark. Suddenly uncomfortable, Mark fidgets with his chair nervously."

Mark, uneasy, responds, "Okay, did we do anything wrong?"

Jaul, in a matter-of-fact tone, says, "I am just hurt and disappointed. We gave you every respect and courtesy."

Mark, "I understand and empathize. I assure you, I will not look at anything I am not supposed to."

Jaul, still not showing any emotion, says, "Fortunately, neither of you did anything wrong, so we won't be disciplining you."

Mark, "Whew, I thought for a moment this was my last day."

Jaul exits the office, "Have a good day, Mark."

Mark returns to his computer. From there, he tinkers with some optional configurations after breaking for lunch. Finally, he checks the Web for new sensor technology before logging off for the day.

Grabbing his keys, Mark makes for his car. The sky is clear and blue; the nearby buildings hide the sun, yet is obviously colorful. The air is clean, slightly warm, and breezy. Reaching his car, he opens the door. Mark shudders as he suddenly detects the same hissing sound he had heard way back when this began. He immediately looks in its direction; he can see nothing there.

The raspy voice says, "You will not stop us. We are coming in as we please."

Mark jumps at the sound of the voice. "Now, now. We will deal with you. It is better for you if you stay on your side of the fence. Tell me where Tina is."

It laughs and hisses a bit. Mark simply exits the parking lot in his Acura. Suddenly, his tablet alerts him of a text. Mark swiftly examines it; it is Isis!

Isis, "Sorry, I missed your calls. I was with my brother. It is a long story."

Mark responds via voice-to-text, "Oh my! Do you want to meet at the Cyberpad and tell me all about it?"

Isis texts back, "Not tonight. I want to, though. How about tomorrow after I rest up?"

The next day after work, Mark sits in the low chair at the Cyberpad and reaches for his energy drink on the glass table. The atmosphere is filled with some computerized dubstep with a hyper-fast beat.

The sliding doors open, and Mark looks up; it is Isis. She is waltzing in; her shimmering black hair bounces yet seems to stick together in near unison. Her bright-green leather jacket tightly grips her upper body and matches quite nicely with her darker yet still-green skirt, which tightly bounces around her knees. She slips off her black leather gloves, then unzips and removes her jacket leisurely, revealing a black rayon top with shimmering-green zigzag pattern. The rayon top has a black zipper that is slightly unzipped, revealing her upper chest. Isis smiles almost seductively as she walks.

"Hi, Mark. Whazzup!" Isis says as she sits down on the nearby chair in a very comfortable, sprawling, leisurely manner.

"Isis! You're here! I have been worried about you for quite some time. I called you frequently, but when you didn't answer, I eventually drove to your place. Your spider was still on-site, yet your apartment was in disarray, with many items removed. So, I called the police," Mark elaborates, partially utilizing hand gestures, "I sent my own minions to seek you out as well."

Isis sighs with a slight smile. "Yeah, thank you so much for your concern. At least someone cares about my welfare!" Not only is he friendly, but he is apparently a good friend, she thought to herself, yet still pondered what Geb had insisted.

"No problem. Now it's your turn. What happened?" Mark smirks loftily.

Isis enthusiastically sits up. "Yes. First, I will order."

Isis looks toward the counter. Mark, smirking, touches his tablet and places the order.

Isis looks at him. "Thank you."

The drink is delivered to their table almost as quickly as they placed the request. Isis grabs her large twenty-four-ounce can and chugs a bit more than a sip. "Ahh."

She turns toward Mark and continues, "Okay, so I woke up that Friday morning and began the usual Friday morning thing when my brother Geb showed up at my door. I was happy to see my brother. However, he had a new friend with him..."

Isis continues recounting the events and finally concludes with, "The police recovered all of our personal effects, and Geb suddenly seemed his usual self again." Isis sighs and relaxes as she ends the story.

Mark looks a bit into the air at seemingly nothing, "Wow! What a story. Did you ever fear the worst? I cannot believe your brother would be so naïve with Sett."

Isis smiles and responds, "Not really; it did not seem like my life was threatened at the time, although I suppose Sett could have walked in with a gun at any time, especially since we were making such intense noise," She pauses then continues, "You know it was obvious that Sett had planned something nefarious because the door on the room we were in only locked from the outside."

Mark slightly nods with a concerned look on his face, "Yeah, the locks were meant to keep someone in rather than out. People who do that typically have bad intentions, such as serial killers and kidnappers."

Isis, "Good thing the police came when they did then."

Mark chugs his energy drink and says, "Did you think perhaps the falcon was there with intent on keeping you company while the police figured it out?"

Isis chuckles with her whole body. "Well, it did seem like a wild bird, so I wasn't sure what its intent was. It was very odd how it seemed to lack fear of us and how it led to our discovery."

They both look up at the giant falcon in the Cyberpad and simultaneously say, "Thank you." After which, they both erupt in laughter.

After a late night with Isis at the Cyberpad, Mark returns home and locates his large, comfortable bed. Quickly shifting to another state of mind, he finds himself in a field of the usual dusty road.

The grassy field stretches out toward the horizon, while behind him lies the beginning of a forest. There is a slight breeze coming from the direction of the dimly lit horizon. A short while away, the luminous cloud is much smaller yet still there. Suddenly, several smaller black gas-like clouds descend upon the field from an unknown location.

Mark quickly generates a sphere of energy and then squeezes it, generating waves of thick energy that assault the small "ghosts." The dark "ghosts" suddenly begin emitting an extremely high-pitched noise that Mark can barely hear. In the distance, the sound of glass cracking and breaking can be heard, presumably from nearby houses.

It barely affects Mark, who is thinking, "Wrong move".

Slamming the ground, large energy waves echo toward the "ghosts." The waves reach the "ghosts" and shred them into a misty substance, which lands on the ground lifelessly. Mark jolts out of surprise when the misty substance reconstitutes back into small clouds as before. They quickly retreat into the distance.

Mark reaches into his pockets and removes several items. An eagle's feather, the symbol of an eye, and the small yet bright luminous orb. He places them on the ground on top of one another. Moving his hands to face each other just above the items on the ground, he spreads them apart and then brings them together, repeatedly waving his arms evenly until his hands connect without touching.

Suddenly, everything flashes a bright amber yellow briefly. Mark slightly stumbles, then regains his composure. He slowly begins to regain visual focus.

Earth, present day.

It looks identical to the setting in one of his video game scenes, but he has seen it before. Somewhere, where was that? Mark strives to recall, was it a dream or a thought?

"Hello?" a female voice says with a very inquisitive tone.

"Who is there?" It is dark outside, and he can see only parts of the tree line.

Mark turns to face the voice. "I-I'm Mark Kheops."

"Oh, I know you—the... the multi-thread guy. I have been reading about you. With the spiders?"

Mark smiles. "Really, you've been reading about me? What did it say?"

Without warning, everything flashes bright amber yellow again, and Mark is standing near the items he had set on the ground.

"It worked! Of all the places and threads that I have been to!" Mark exclaims.

"Now, if only I can make it work for a bit longer, I'll have completed my objective of finally utilizing this amazing ability," Mark continues, thinking as he picks up his symbols.

Placing them in his pocket, Mark cannot help but notice that the portal from which the black ooze had come is gone. "Awesome. I had no interest in visiting them. I am not even sure how that portal opened. Hopefully, it is closed, he thought to himself. I must try to ensure that I don't open portals like that."

Mark wakes and looks at the window, the morning light blasting through.

Reaching his tablet, Mark quickly texts Garrick, "I had an encounter with black ghosts in the dreamscape."

After ten minutes, while Mark relaxes in bed before starting the day, Garrick responds with a text. "Really, what happened?"

Mark exuberantly responds, "Well, it was a fight, and they retreated."

Garrick's delayed response, "Wow! Lol"

Chapter 13

Closure and Revelation

Mark relocates his leather trench coat, allowing him to exit his vehicle more easily. After which, he slips into the building and makes for the coffee machine. Today, he should have his prototype for testing. Even though he did not care that much, these people are associated with people who are stealing from him and abducting his friends after all. It is better to learn 'what he can' from the inside than to quit.

Large coffee in hand, Mark waltzes down the hallway to the manufacturing lab. Swiping his badge, Mark opens the door and swiftly finds his way to the work order desk. Again, he swipes his badge and taps the screen where the selection for his project is. Turning quickly, Mark sits down on the simple yet elegant chairs lined up along the wall for waiting.

An engineer in a large white cloak approaches the desk, and then leaning on the desk, the engineer looks directly at him. "Mark, I presume."

Mark smiles casually. "Yes, that's me."

Glancing at the screen and then again at Mark, he says, "Unfortunately, all prototype production has been put on standby. For now, you will have to wait. Please discuss this with your project manager. Have a good day!" With that, the engineer swiftly exits the room without looking at Mark.

Mark is a little taken aback by that. What the? Mark swiftly returns to his desk and loads up his computer.

"Nothing unusual here," Mark mumbles sarcastically to himself.

He checks his calendar; all is still normal, and there are no cancellations on it. Finishing his coffee, Mark slips down the hallway. Approaching Dacian's office, the door is open. Dacian can sense that Mark is approaching.

"Come in, come in." Dacian gestures with his hands, his eyes meandering.

"I have been advised there will be no prototype production. Is there something I need to know?" Mark queries, a bit unsure.

Dacian shows perspiration on his forehead as he wipes his nose. After a momentary pause, Dacian responds with a sigh, "The project is suspended for now. I was going to inform you tomorrow, yet I understand you have discovered it before I could. Right now, this company is in for a rough ride and may not make it. All future projects are suspended until further notice."

Mark turns serious, "Uh, my contract is suspended? You know that according to the contract, you can only do that during financial difficulty for up to two months before the contract self-terminates with a small single-pay period compensation?"

Dacian looks down at the papers on his desk and then responds, "You know your contract! For now, we will make use of that clause in the contract, and we will let you know if we need to terminate the contract. That is the best I can do for now. Leave any company project files in the usual places on the hard drive. You can go for now."

That was a quick day at work; he had barely finished his coffee. Mark reaches for the door and steps outside. There is no noticeable difference at the office except that the parking lot shows fewer cars than usual for this time of day. The air is still, and the noise is minimal. A few light, wispy clouds populate the otherwise blue sky, as if remnants of a high-speed travel path. There seem to be a few birds chirping in the distance.

Opening the car door, Mark positions himself in the driver's seat in one smooth motion. Mark felt a little more aware for some reason. There is a placid sense in the air, and it seems Mark can sense every detail of his surroundings. He pauses for an "in the moment" reflection, slips his key chip in the ignition, and swiftly returns home.

Pulling into the neat yet slightly dusty garage, Mark exits the car and, in a civil manner, waltzes through the door. He could not help but notice the empty spot, like a void, where the three-dimensional art previously resided. The echo of its previous existence serves as a reminder, making the room appear incomplete. How annoying, he thinks as he quickly locates a statue of a purposely smooth, chiseled, and un-frilled Falcon to take its place.

"There, that's better," Mark mumbles to himself.

Turning to the den, he grabs the controller and turns his home entertainment system on. After which, he quickly reaches for a scoop of gourmet coffee. Standing at the coffee maker, awaiting his coffee, he ponders what will come of the ghosts now while the news plays in the background.

Mark sips his coffee and turns his attention to the daily news when his tablet alerts him of an incoming text.

It is Ramses. "Guess what? The police have located my property!"

Mark texts back, "Awesome, is Garrick with you?"

Ramses replies, "Yes, Garrick and I are here. What's the scene there?"

Mark texts back while sipping his steaming coffee, "Well, my contract is suspended for now. Can I check your scene?"

Ramses text replies, "See you soon!"

Mark finishes the coffee while grabbing his jacket and making for the door.

Mark swiftly drives a few blocks down the road; the nice thing is that Ramses lives nearby. Ramses' enormous curved driveway is nearly a parking lot, where the gray concrete has large edges colored with a golden tan. The surrounding lawn has lush, thickly-bladed Bermuda grass, which intermixes with palm trees and sand. Stepping out of his Acura, Mark walks toward the front door; the multi-pathed walkway alone is as large as a four-lane highway. The walkway is a golden sand-colored concrete with a central bronze-colored marble pyramid. The pyramid features a constant stream of steaming water pouring from the top into the surrounding pool, adding a nice misty effect to the surrounding air.

The house has sizeable golden concrete blocks that appear three stories high, even though they are only two. The large glass door, with a faded bronze handle, is tinted, purposely looking old even though it is relatively new. Mark reaches for the obvious touchpad on the door and touches it, causing a barely audible custom ringtone to sound from the inside.

Ramses opens the door and says, "Hey, whazzup!"

"What's the flow?" Mark replies, smiling, as he enters the foyer.

The foyer has a marble-tiled floor with a naturally lit Plexiglas ceiling nearly thirty feet high.

Garrick smiles widely. "Want some pizza? We're watching an action flick while we return Ramses' things to where they go."

The three meander into the enormous den, which is colored with various creams, whites, and blacks. In the center, a large quantity of boxes and furniture rests on the plush, velvety cream carpeting.

Scanning the room, Mark comments, "'Do,' your dominion always seems so colossal even when it is small."

Ramses smirks widely, a small tear forming, ending with a chuckle. "What can I say? It's my magic essence!"

Then Mark turns to Ramses, laughing nearly to tears. "They really ran off with a lot of stuff. Really, they took all that?"

Ramses smirks and reaches for his head. "I know. I was a bit distraught. You should have seen it before the movers brought it back!"

Moving ever so slowly, the sun begins to spray the den while luminous rays cause the entire room to look like some old museum or cream-colored tomb.

Mark pours himself a Whiskey-Seven, then looks at Ramses. "So, what's the story?"

Ramses relaxes in a velvety chair and reaches for his drink. "Apparently, some thieving ring has been rounded up. Fortunately for me, they arrested them before they could liquidate my personal belongings. Much more fortunate was my insurance company!" He smirks. They all laugh at that briefly. They spent the evening assisting Ramses with reorganizing his house.

Mark exits the house and walks towards his car. The moonlight dances on the steaming water fountain as if moving to some rhythm. The air is breezy and warm, with a hint of tropical foliage reaching his nostrils. The quick jaunt home was uneventful, and no one else was on the road.

SpiderSilk

Groggily awakening from what seems like a deep sleep, all Tina can see is blackness.

"What happened? Did I fall?" She thought to herself.

She can hear some whispering voices nearby. Slowly, she can make out some forms in the darkness; it appears to be the basement. How did she get here? She slowly becomes aware that she is surrounded by dark, cloud-like forms saying various things to each other.

One states to her, "You've crossed the threshold." It reaches out and touches her head. Suddenly, she lost her sight completely.

"Until now, I actually liked this place better than Olympus; I could start young again and everything." Gasping, she touches her eyes and can still not see anything. Is she blind? Just like that?

All the black clouds start snickering, and one says, "After we're finished reprogramming you, you'll never know the difference. This will be fun for us; I can't say the same for you. You had the wrong ally. Mark's kind is not welcome around these parts."

A strange sensation overcame her head, cold and slightly painful like a headache. She suddenly lost consciousness.

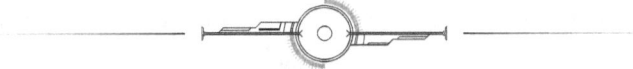

Reaching his house, Mark felt slightly different than usual and had felt that way all day. It is like he can sense every placid and active detail in the atmosphere; a sense of inner satisfaction makes him feel extraordinarily enthusiastic for the coming day. Mark reaches his comfortable, large bed and relaxes. He is apparently tired because he very quickly shifts into the dream state.

Mark's Dream, Morning in Braila, Vular.

Mark finds himself drifting through a town. The environment is a bit unusual, and Mark has less control over his movement. Mark drifts into a hospital. The echoes of doctors and patients reverberate through the gleaming white hallway. Suddenly, Mark realizes he cannot control himself, unlike in other dreams, and he involuntarily drifts into a hospital room.

Several people in essential attire are standing around, some praying while others announcing something about the gods. A doctor and a nurse in the usual white outfits stand near a bed, having a plastic curtain pulled entirely out of the way. Approaching, he can finally understand what they are saying.

One man says, "He flatlined! Is he going to die? All this time, he has been in a coma. For some reason, I assumed he would eventually awaken."

A woman says, "God help him!"

The doctor, holding a clipboard, looks at the man and responds, "There was no real sign that he would die, and we have been doing everything we can to bring him out of the coma."

Mark moves into position, floating above where he can see the man in the bed. Mark quickly recognizes him; he is Chris Vocal, CEO of Applied Dynamics. Chris looks peacefully asleep, resting underneath the blue fuzzy blanket in his hospital bed. Multiple health machines are littered around the bed. Some for metrics, some as tools. The warm sun illuminates the room where Chris is apparently fighting for his life.

Mark looks up above Chris's head at what he thought was a clock but is shocked to see it is something else entirely. Above Chris's bed is a dreamcatcher, the same dreamcatcher from a previous dream with the keyhole and everything. Mark recalls the key he used on the dreamcatcher previously but no longer knows where it may be.

Looking at the measurements, he notices the flat line replacing the active.

The man exclaims, "Without warning, flatline!"

The doctor looks at him in a very serious manner. "I understand; we are doing all we can."

A nurse is administering a syringe to his feeder.

Suddenly, the measurements come to life. The nurse jolts out of shock. Chris's finger twitches a bit, and his eyes began rolling under his eyelids. The man wearing some basic blue jeans, a T-shirt, and a baseball cap, who had spoken recently, asks with an emotional inflection in his tone, "Is he going to make it, or is it his last gasp?"

Quickly, the nurse begins to check his eyes. Chris starts spastic-ally jolting, and then his measurements normalize.

The doctor exuberantly exclaims, "I think he is going to make it!"

Everyone in the room says, "Thank the gods!"

Nearly without warning, Chris opens his eyes. "Wh-wh-where am I?" he says.

Chris's eyes roll around like they are not reporting to the mind. Apparently, Chris is still blind.

"Oh my god!" The man who had been talking previously nearly fell over.

The doctor, clearly in shock, quickly comes around. "Hi, Chris. You're in the Braila Hospital. You were in a plane accident a while ago, and you've been in a coma."

The nurse jabs, "Glad to have you back. You scared us for a minute there. We thought we were going to lose you."

Chris relaxes in bed and says, "I had the weirdest dreams, like a bad dream."

The nurse says, "I'm not surprised."

Chris continues, "I was in some place called Olympus, where my company was faltering… I… I had some powerful opponents, including a quantum eye that was only beginning to develop."

An elderly gentleman expresses shock, "That is the scariest thing I've heard in a long time. You have quite the active imagination."

One of the women interjects, "It's over now. You're here with us, back home in Braila."

SpiderSilk

Mark begins to drift away from the hospital room when a loud noise interrupts him. Mark forcefully opens his eyes to the usual patterns in the ceiling.

Mark sits up at the edge of the bed while turning off the alarm on his tablet. Light blasts in, causing natural warmth to permeate most of the room. Mark takes a moment to look around the room. Everything is as he had left it. Everything seems so real; it must be real.

Mark closes his eyes briefly and then opens them again. This time, his third eye opens with them. Mark scrutinizes what he is viewing; the imagery is sharp and clear, and nothing is warped. In fact, his senses are a bit more acute, and he can see details beyond what he would have normally detected. He can see all sorts of energies, including a large quantity of spiders like in a previous dream. Standing, his third eye closes as he makes for the kitchen.

Mark recalls the dream. "What a trip," he mumbles while enjoying the velvety carpet. Meandering down the stairs, Mark reaches the den, where he clicks his television system on. Today is one of the first days in a long time that Mark did not have a contract to work on. The news immediately starts playing while Mark grabs a scoop of espresso. The aroma of the espresso mixes with Mark's natural masculinity and the still-fresh carpet smell, which has been there since he had the carpets cleaned.

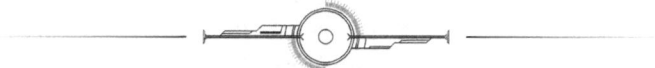

Mark is sipping his espresso when his tablet alerts him of a text. The television news shifts to breaking news. "Chris Vocal, CEO and owner of Applied Dynamics was found deceased this morning. We are still determining the cause of death; it seems he suddenly fainted at the moment."

While checking his tablet, Mark says to himself, "I hope that isn't a bad omen."

"Call me when you have a moment," It's a text from Ben.

Suddenly, an actual call is coming in, and Mark answers it.

"Mark? This is Dacian from Applied Dynamics. We will be terminating your contract. You will get your promised paycheck. Applied Dynamics is going into liquidation after the death of our owner and CEO. It was nice meeting you." Dacian has a very matter-of-fact tone, and there is no video.

Mark replies, "Okay, I kind of had a feeling that things weren't as great as they could be. Thank you for letting me know."

"Have a good day," Dacian finalizes the conversation and then hangs up.

Mark sips his espresso with a moment of warmth, then calls Ben. "Hello, Ben. How are you on this fine day?" Mark zaps with a smile.

Ben smirks jovially. "Well, Applied Dynamics apparently has termed your contract."

Mark chuckles. "Yes, I was on the phone with them only moments ago. Not every company liquidates after the owner chokes."

Ben, serious yet still smiling, says, "Yeah, that is true. That company is quickly dissolving. You have plenty of funds on hand, though, don't you? I doubt you're shakin' in your boots!"

Mark wipes his forehead in jest, still smirking. "I'm fine, and I have more money than before, actually."

Ben chuckles. "Okay, how about you take a break and enjoy it? When you're ready, give me a call. I'll have some prime contract options, and I believe Rae is interested in alternative business options."

Mark smirks. "Will do, will do, friend."

Mark jolts by the interruption of an intruder.

"Hello, good morning, beautiful!" Mairis announces.

Mark braces himself against the counter. "Oh… good morning to come over since my contract is terminated."

Mairis smiles confidently. "You'll have a new contract, I assume?"

Mark makes a slow, beaming smirk. "Apparently, I'll have some prime options. But first, I'll take a nice break to enjoy my new house and money."

Mairis touches her mouth while stepping back with a slightly seductive look. "That's what we need to do then. I am down for whatever!"

Later that night, Mark was comfortably sleeping in his bed when he suddenly awoke to a growl similar to the one he had heard previously. Reaching for his eyes, he rubbed them as his body transitioned from the dream state. Another growl came from across the room.

Swiftly, Mark shifts his legs off the edge of the bed as he sits up. The growl turns to a whimper. The room is extremely dark, more so than usual. Mark opens his eyes, which are a bright, vibrant white light—no pupils, just pure light. The whimpering turns into a quiet yelp.

Mark responds to animal noises, "That's right. There is something to fear in the dark... me."

SpiderSilk

Afterword

Many of the scenarios in this book come from actual dream and non-dream experiences. This story has been formatted to be interesting, and I hope you liked it. Preferably, it has inspired you with the possibilities of what may be, where we can be, and where we have been. While we all create our own little universe, there are those universes designed by others that we will want to interact with and those that we do not. Plan wisely, but don't leave out the thrill of connecting.

www.ingramcontent.com/pod-product-compliance
Lightning Source LLC
LaVergne TN
LVHW040049080526
838202LV00045B/3550